ONE GOLD HEART

DOMINANT CORD, BOOK 1

SADIE HALLER

QTP

ISBN-13: 978-0993826436

ISBN-10: 0993826431

ABOUT THIS BOOK

Finn Taylor is an asshole. So why does he keep showing up in Mac's late-night fantasies as the Dom of her dreams? She can't even ignore him, because she's stuck working with the fellow musician for the Christmas concert season.

Mac Wallis is a mess, and Finn can't fall for a submissive who's so damaged she needs medication just to get through a performance. But he's drawn to the beautiful oboist, even as he keeps pissing her off. He can't resist trying to take care of her—in every way.

~ Books by Sadie Haller ~

Dominant Cord
One Gold Heart
One Gold Knot
One Gold Triquetra

Tainted Pearl
Tainted Pearl
Tainted Shadow

Frisky Beavers
Prime Minister
Dr. Bad Boy
Full Mountie
Mr. Hat Trick (coming 2017)

For my amazing Grandma.
I miss you every day, but especially at Christmas.

ONE

Mac checked the caller ID and grinned as she answered, "Hi, Sully."

"I need a huge favour."

"I'm quite certain it's customary to at least say hello, maybe even engage in a little small talk before making requests," Mac scolded.

"Look Mac, I'm desperate and I don't have time to suck up. I was stupid and went on a date yesterday to the outdoor skating rink, and—"

Mac interrupted. "But you can't skate."

"Yeah, back to the 'I was stupid' part. Anyway, I broke two ribs when I crashed into the side railing and I'm out of commission for the next six weeks."

"I'd have more sympathy if you'd stop thinking with your dick, you know."

"I don't need sympathy, just a favour. Dominant Cord has gigs booked for most of December, starting Friday, and I need you to sub for me."

Mac cringed. "Tell me you don't mean Friday, as in day after tomorrow Friday."

"Yes, that's exactly the Friday I mean."

"Bugger. You, of all people, know I hate performing. There must be someone else you can call on."

"'Fraid not. Everybody's booked solid. C'mon Mac, you know I wouldn't ask this of you if I had any other option."

"You are such a weasel."

"I knew I could count on you."

Mac was suspicious. "Hang on, what are we playing?"

"Bach's Christmas Oratorio," Sully mumbled.

"For that, you miserable lump of knob cheese you are paying for the beta-blockers and you owe me a favour to be named later."

"Done."

"Shit, that was too easy. I have a couple of errands to run this morning. I'll swing by to pick up the music and get the details from you on my way home."

"Fabulous. I'll see you soon."

"Yeah, just feckin' fabulous," Mac muttered as she hung up the phone.

MAC RANG THE BELL, nervously clenching her fists as she waited. Minutes later, she took another anxious look at her watch and rechecked the house number against the address Sully had given her. Yup, apparently, this was the place. She rang the bell again and waited. Irritated and out of patience, she decided to make one last effort before giving up. As she prepared to knock, the door was replaced by a broad chest and impressive biceps accentuated by a muscle-hugging, black t-shirt. She stomped on her lust. She was here to work, and didn't need to complicate her life any further.

"What?"

Mac took an involuntary step back and looked way up. She briefly regarded his handsome face, but his Guiness-brown eyes had her wet and tingly before she could regain her composure. She extended her hand and said, "Um, hi. I'm Mac Wallis, Sully's sub."

The man gave her the once over and blew out an exasperated breath. "You've got the date wrong, pet. The play party isn't until Sunday night."

His deep voice resonated within Mac's chest, sending another trickle of moisture into her panties. "Sunday? Sully told me we were scheduled to play on Friday night."

"I don't think so, pet. We're otherwise engaged on Friday. Where is Sully, anyway? He should have been here ten minutes ago."

"He's at home, where else would he be?"

"Here. He is supposed to be here for a rehearsal, dammit"

Realisation dawned and Mac held up her index finger. "Hang on a mo." She suspected this man wasn't often interrupted by a finger waving woman, and his surprised look amused her. She reached into her bag, pulled out her phone, and punched in Sully's number.

She didn't wait for his greeting before laying into him. "That favour to be named later just doubled, pal. I'm standing in front of a very grumpy man who wants to know why you're not here and I am. I'll be generous and assume you are loopy on pain meds and forgot. I'm going to give the phone to Mr. Peevy-pants, and you will rectify the situation immediately."

Mac handed the phone over and stomped off the porch, needing the space to cool off. She was already so stressed about having to play for strangers on crappy reeds, she didn't need to colour it with anger and arousal. Bugger that feckin' weasel, Sully, anyway. She kept her back to the house as she inhaled deeply through her nose, letting each breath trickle from her mouth.

She was almost calm when Mr. Sexy-voice invaded her happy place. "Mac, he wants a quick word."

She turned slowly and took one more deep breath before heading back up the stairs to reclaim her phone. "This had better be fixed, because if there is even the slightest problem, I'm done. Are we clear?"

"I am SO sorry, Mac. Really, I meant to call and—"

"I don't want excuses, Sully. Just tell me it's sorted."

"It's sorted."

Mac disconnected, and returned the phone to her bag.

"That was rude. You didn't even say goodbye."

Mac's eyes flashed as she wagged her finger again. "Stop right there. I am doing him a huge favour. Far bigger than I think you could ever understand. His fuck-up increased the value of that favour and we've been friends long enough that we don't always have to observe telephone etiquette. I am here as Sully's substitute because he is unable to play. Can I assume we are both on the same page, now? "

"Yes, we're on the same page, and if it makes you feel any better, I did give him shit for not giving me a heads-up. I'm sorry for the misunderstanding. Perhaps we can start again?"

Mac nodded and extended her hand. "Hi, I'm Mac Wallis, and I'm here to substitute for Sully while he is incapacitated."

The man took it and said, "Nice to meet you Mac. I'm Finn Taylor, and I play flute. I appreciate you agreeing to step in for Sully and help us out. Come on inside and meet the rest of the group."

Mac followed Finn into the house. She removed her

shoes and set her bags on the floor before shrugging out of her coat. Finn took it from her as she slid her arms free, and hung it on the coat tree in the corner.

"The music room is at the back of the house. We'll swing through the kitchen and get you some water on the way."

"Thanks."

"So, where and when did you and Sully meet?"

Mac had to cut him off right there. Her attraction to Finn was already problematic, fostering any kind of personal connection would be a disaster. "Look, Finn, I'm here to do a job, nothing more."

Finn grabbed a glass from the cupboard and set it on the counter before fetching the jug of filtered water from the fridge. "Okay, no personal stuff. How about professional? I trust Sully to send us someone capable, but what are your credentials?" He asked, as he filled her glass.

"I got my Bachelor of Music in performance from McGill," Mac stated in a tone that declared the subject closed.

Apparently, Finn had other ideas. "And...?"

"And, that's it."

"That takes care of educational, what about professional?"

"I don't play professionally. I hate performing. Like I said, this is a huge favour for Sully."

Finn returned the jug to the fridge and paused a moment before turning to face her. "What on earth was Sully thinking? How are you going to manage our concert schedule if you hate performing?"

Mac lifted her chin and looked him dead in the eye. "Sully was thinking he was down to his very last, desperate hope. And I will manage with the help of beta-blockers."

"Sweet, sweaty Jesus, what a cluster-fuck," Finn muttered as he stalked to the music room.

———

"BRACE YOURSELVES," Finn shouted just before he and Mac entered. "Sully's gone and busted a couple of ribs, his replacement doesn't play professionally, and the icing on the cake? She requires drugs to perform."

He took a brief look at the trio of shocked faces before he continued. "This is Mac Wallis." He shifted his attention back to Mac, mildly curious at her wary, sideways glance at the piano. He pointed to an empty chair. "You can sit there." He introduced the rest of the quintet, pointing to each in turn. "That's Jack Riley on bassoon, Wilson Kennedy on clarinet, and Griff Edwards on horn." Not giving anyone an opportunity to do more than nod in greeting, Finn carried on. "Now let's get started. We're already running late. Mac, how long until your reeds will be ready to play?"

Mac settled into her chair. She immediately opened her instrument case and tucked the top-joint of her oboe into her armpit while she continued with her preparations. "I soaked them before I left, so they should be good to go as soon as I have my top-joint warmed up. Give me two or three minutes to get myself organised?"

"Like I have a fucking choice."

Mac stopped what she was doing and glared at Finn, her eyes bright with hurt and indignation. Then she unloaded. "Look, I've had just about enough of the snide, snarky bullshit. You don't want me here. I get it. I don't want me here either, but the way I see it, you've got three options. You find someone else to replace Sully, you cancel all your gigs until he's better, or you deal with me. I'll give you until the end of this rehearsal to make your decision, but I will not put up with any more of your unprofessional behaviour. Just because I don't sing for my supper, don't get the idea that you can treat me with any less respect than you would Sully."

Ignoring the audience, Finn replied, "Fair point. Are you just about ready to start?"

"Absofeckinglutely."

"Okay, let's do a full run-through without stopping, then we'll see what we have to work with."

Finn kept an eye on Mac throughout the rehearsal, ready to cue her the moment she got lost. To his relief, the opportunity never came. She played perfectly. Instruments were laid to rest with the death of the final note, and applause quickly replaced the stunned silence.

Jack gave Mac a quick wink. "Well, Finn, I know which option I'm voting for."

Finn was surprised by the unfamiliar feeling of jealousy. Where had that come from?

Wilson piped up. "Well done, Mac. I have to know, was that straight sight reading, or have you played this before?"

"I played it years ago at university, but not since. I had hoped to have time to go over it before coming to rehearsal, but with a concert on Friday, making reeds was my priority."

Finn finally found his voice. "You played it well here in rehearsal conditions, but I'm concerned about how you'll do in performance, especially when you're drugged up."

"Knock it off, Finn," Griff snapped. "If Sully trusts Mac and her abilities enough to send her to us as his replacement, I think we need to accept she'll be fine."

"I'm just uncomfortable about people relying on performance enhancing drugs."

"I guess Viagra's not an option for you then," Mac snapped.

The others sniggered as Finn's eyes flashed, but Mac didn't back down. "This may have been just a rehearsal for you, but for me, it was worse than a performance. In a performance, I'm playing for strangers who are there to enjoy the music. Here, I was playing for strangers who were looking to pick apart every little thing. Now, I'm tired, grumpy, and ready to go home. So, what's your decision, Finn?"

"I still don't like that you use drugs, but we have no choice. You're in."

"You make it sound like I'm a crack-head. If you can come up with a drug-free way for me to cope with my performance anxiety, I'm all ears. Not that it's any of your business, Mr. Just-Say-No, but the beta-blockers were the absolute last resort for me. Without them, I wouldn't have graduated from university. Now, if we're done here, I'm going home."

"Yeah, we're done. Same time tomorrow night. I'll need your contact information. Phone numbers and email, please. Here's mine." Finn handed over a business card.

Mac grabbed her wallet from her purse and slipped his card into one of the compartments, before pulling out one of her own. "Here." She slapped the card down on the seat next to her and proceeded to stow her gear.

As they packed up, the rest of the quintet watched the sparks fly between Finn and Mac. They said their farewells, and Finn didn't miss the look of panic in Mac's eyes as the others left en-mass.

He crouched next to her, bothered by her obvious distress. "I'm sorry, I'm not making a very good impression. I'm angry at the situation, and I've been taking it out on you. I'm not usually this much of an asshole. You were great tonight, and I look forward to playing with you." He left out the part about his wish for an alternative because her need for medication completely freaked him out.

"You're forgiven. I'm sorry too. It's not like I've been all sweetness and light. And before you blame it on the beta-blockers, I've been every shade of pissed off since I got that call from Sully this morning. The beta-blockers didn't make their appearance until just before I headed over here. Now, I really do need to get going."

Finn stood to give her space while he watched her gather her belongings and scurry out the door. Sully would be getting a call as soon as she was gone. Fucker.

"What the fuck, man," Finn bellowed, "You sent us a drug addicted amateur."

"Bullshit. I sent you one of the best oboists I know. The only reason she's not on my sub-list, let alone at the top of it, is her crippling performance anxiety. Trust me, if I'd had any other options, I wouldn't have done this to her."

"Seriously? Done this to her? What about what you've done to us? We're going to crash and burn out there."

"You can't tell me that she wasn't perfection itself, so what's really got your boxers in a braid?"

"I admit it, she played beautifully. Pitch perfect, and not a note out of place. But she needs drugs to play. I can't deal with that."

"No, she doesn't need drugs to play. She needs prescription medication to perform. She was fine when we first started university, but as the music became more difficult, and the performance requirements more demanding, she developed anxiety so unmanageable, we couldn't get her on stage. She could get to the wings, but then she'd just sink to the floor and shake. She hates performing because she hates taking beta-blockers. I doubt you're going to believe me, but I'll say it anyway, Mac does not require medication for anxiety outside of performance situations. So, do me a favour, try to put aside your own issues, and accept that she's willing to put aside hers to help us out. Oh, and for the record, the only way she's going to make you crash and burn, is if she changes her mind about playing. It seems to me, you are the only one who is likely to make that happen."

"Way to make me feel like even more of an asshole."

"Oh shit, what did you do?"

"I was angry. I'm still angry, but I was angry and I took it out on her."

"Way to go, Finn."

"Well, a heads up before she showed at my door declaring herself as your submissive might have been helpful."

"Back up. What do you mean, declaring herself as my submissive?"

"I opened the door, and she said, 'I'm Mac, I'm Sully's sub.' Fuck, man, I thought she was yet another in your impressive collection of ditzy subs and she'd got the day of the play party wrong."

"Ow, ow, fucking ow. Fuck, don't make me laugh, please don't tell me any more. At least not until I am under the full effects of really good pain meds. Seriously, you thought I would have a sub of mine show up to a play party alone?"

"It didn't seem like you, but with such a restricted guest-list, I wasn't sure.

"Now you can be sure. There is no way I would let a sub show up anywhere to play without me."

"A little late, but good to know. I guess I really have some sucking up to do."

"Yup. And because I like you, I'm going to give you some helpful tips."

MAC CALLED SULLY AS SOON as she got home. "I'm so feckin' mad at you, I could break every single reed you have and leave you with nothing but commercial student reeds to perform on."

"I'm sorry, Mac. I fucked up. I get it. Now stop busting my balls and tell me how it went."

"Great. Between your buddy mistaking me for one of your bondage-bunnies and accusing me of being a drug addict, my evening was complete."

"Okay, you've made your point, things aren't exactly smooth between you and Finn, but personal friction aside, how did rehearsal go?"

"It went fine. Fortunately, they're doing something I've played before, even if it was forever ago. Thank fuck I didn't have to sight-read."

"I knew it'd work out. There's another rehearsal tomorrow night, right?"

"Yeah. I'm struggling on whether to take blockers this time. Tonight was a no-brainer, but I hate taking them unless I absolutely have to."

"Why don't you hold off, but have them with you so you can take one if you find you need it. Maybe just knowing they're there will be enough for you to manage without."

"Yeah, I guess I could do that, but if I do end up needing them, I don't want to waste everyone else's time while I wait for them to take effect."

"I wouldn't worry. They are concert-ready, and they'll be happy enough with a little extra gossip time while your meds kick in. Are you okay, now?"

"Yeah, I'm calmer, and a little less angry with you, but that doesn't let you off the hook. You are into me for two, count 'em, two favours to be named later."

"Yeah, yeah, I know, and I'm sure you'll take every opportunity to remind me."

"Of course I will. Right, I'm going to bed now. I'm wiped. Good night. I hope your ribs start to feel better really soon."

"Thanks. G'night, Mac."

MAC STARED into the dark as she stroked her cat, Gounod. He was settled in his usual spot, full length between her legs with his head and front paw resting on her upper thigh. She'd tried every technique for falling asleep she could think of, but her mind would not shut off. She kept thinking back to Finn, and wondered how she could possibly be attracted to such an asshole?

It's not like he comes across as the sexy bad-boy type, either. He may believe otherwise, but he's just an asshole, plain and simple. He accused her of being a drug addict and treated her like she was some skid-row junkie. That alone should have killed all feeling in her girly-bits. Nothing turned her off faster than humiliation, but damn, if this guy didn't seem to work some kind of hoo-hoo voodoo.

And with that thought, her pussy was swollen and needy, and she wasted no time giving in to its demand. Gounod growled his outrage as she shifted him out of her way. Mac rolled her eyes and laughed. "Suck it up you big baby, you can come back later when I'm done taking care of the other pussy in my life." She reached into the drawer of her bedside table for her Rabbit. She slid it into her eager cunt and flipped the switch to nirvana. Three orgasms later, she drifted into a fitful sleep.

FINN STOOD in the shower and let the spray envelop him like a warm blanket as he thought back through his evening. Damn she was cute. Even standing at full height, her mop of dark, curly hair would barely skim the bottom of his chin. He first noticed her soulful eyes, but it was that sassy mouth of hers that was going to get him into trouble.

The little head sure didn't care if she was a druggie. From the moment he'd opened the door, his cock was fully present and accounted for. Thank fuck he'd gone for the tighty-whities and loose fitting trousers. The last thing he needed was the rest of the guys riding him over a tent-pole in his pants.

Finn fisted his erection and stroked it from root to tip as he imagined Mac's luscious pink lips wrapped around him. Taking him deep, swallowing him whole. His breathing increased, his heart pounded. After sporting an erection for hours, the image of Mac on her knees and his cock down her throat had him exploding with a speed he hadn't experienced since he'd watched his first porn film as a teenager.

Once he'd finally made it to bed, Finn carefully considered each of Sully's suggestions for fixing things with Mac.

TWO

Mac checked the caller ID and groaned before answering. "Hello?"

"Mac, hi, it's Finn."

Mac tried to keep the wariness from her voice as she responded. "Yes?"

"I was wondering if you could come over a little early tonight?"

"Why?"

"You said if I had any ideas on how to keep you from needing beta-blockers, you were all ears."

"I am all ears, and you have one of them right now, so, how about you tell me what you have in mind."

"I'd rather talk in person. You'll be coming over anyway, so, unless you have other plans you can't reschedule, what can it hurt? I was thinking you could join me for dinner. It would be refreshing to cook for more than just myself."

Mac didn't bother to hide her irritation. "Look Finn, you don't approve of me, and I don't like you. I'm doing a favour for a friend, and that's as far as it goes. I appreciate that you've been giving thought to an alternative way to deal with my performance anxiety, but as far as I know, I've tried it all, and the reality is, I don't trust you. You have a hang-up. That's not my problem."

"Mac, I'm sorry I've given you reason not to trust that I'm working in your best interests, but maybe you could try trusting that I'm working in mine, and my hang-up could provide you with an alternative to medication."

"No. I'll be there and ready to play by seven. That is the extent of my obligation to Sully, and by extension, to you. I have a busy day ahead, so if there is nothing else?"

"No, I don't think so."

"Fine, then I'll see you this evening, goodbye"

"Bye."

MAC OPENED the text without checking who sent it.

'Open your front door.'

A quick look at her inbox confirmed it was from Sully. What was he up to? She opened the door to a small basket of goodies from her favourite chocolate shop and smiled. She picked up the basket and brought it inside, feeling no urgency to read the card. Experience told her Sully was sorry, and chocolate consumption always took priority.

She ripped the cellophane from the basket and sorted the chocolates in order of preference. As usual, she started with her least favourites, and finished with the ones she liked best. She popped the first chocolate into her mouth before grabbing the envelope and removing the card it contained. As she read, the confection turned to mud in her mouth and she promptly spit it into the discarded wrapping. She grabbed her phone and punched in Sully's number.

"You rat-bastard. You feckin', sneaky, wasted sper—"

"Hold on, Mac. Just hear me out, okay? Please?" Sully took advantage of the brief silence and continued. "Finn fucked up. He knows he fucked up, and he's just looking for a chance to make it as right as possible. I feel partially responsible for this mess, so I need to do what I can to help fix it."

"Deceiving me is not how you fix things, Sully. You sent that text. You deliberately led me to believe those chocolates were from you. How am I supposed to trust you when you'd do something like this?"

"Yeah, I sent the text to ensure you would open the door. I should have known you would assume the package was from me, but I didn't deliberately mislead you. I'm sorry, sweetie. I hate the effect my lack of caution is having on you. Who'd have thought an afternoon skating date would have such crazy consequences."

"Fucker."

"Here's the thing, I think both you and Finn overreacted, and we need to get some kind of truce in place before tonight's rehearsal. I know you turned down supper at Finn's, but how about I order in and you two meet here, in somewhat neutral territory?"

"You'll be there, too?"

"Of course."

Mac considered everything Sully'd said, and after being friends for so many years, she knew he would never do anything deliberately to jeopardise their relationship. Besides, with the demanding concert schedule ahead of her, the last thing she needed was tension between herself and a fellow musician. "Fine." Mac huffed. "I'll be there at five and there had better be Indian."

"Great. I'll give Finn a call and I'll see you at five."

Mac stabbed the end button and threw her phone on

the sofa as she thought about what to do with the chocolates. The peevish part of her wanted to package them back up and return them to Finn, but the rest of her wanted to cue up a DVD and gorge herself on them while she worked on reeds. With a concert the following night, it would be a struggle to have performance-worthy reeds ready in time. Her love of chocolate won out, and she settled in for a reed-making marathon with her buddies, chocolate, and The Doctor.

It was Finn who opened the door when Mac arrived at Sully's house. "Oh, hi. Um, thanks for the chocolates, I enjoyed them." Mac stepped inside, kicked off her shoes and hung her coat on a hook behind the door. "They're my favourites, but you already knew that."

"Hi, yourself, and you're welcome." There was a twinkle in Finn's eyes as he asked, "Did you enjoy them all?"

"Of course I did. I have virtually no self-control when it comes to good chocolate. No, to be perfectly honest, I have absolutely no self-control when it comes to chocolate of any kind."

"Tell me that's not all you ate today."

"Do you really want me to tell you that, or do you want me to tell you the truth."

Finn flipped his gaze skyward and shook his head in disbelief. "Well, at least you'll be having a somewhat healthy supper before rehearsal. It arrived just a few minutes ago. How about you join Sully in the dining room and I'll bring the food through?"

"Okay, but I don't mind giving you a hand."

"No, no, you go ahead and get yourself settled at the table, I'll be in with the food in no time."

Mac stepped into the dining room and greeted her friend. "Hey, how are you feeling?"

"Well, I've certainly been better. How about you?"

She leaned down and laid a gentle kiss on the top of Sully's head before settling herself in the chair to his right. "I've been better too, but at least all my ribs are intact."

"Well, that's something, isn't it?"

"Here we go." Finn set two dishes on the table. "Start serving yourselves and I'll be back with the rest."

Mac picked up Sully's plate and started loading it. Noting his raised eyebrows, she admonished, "Don't you get any funny ideas, bucko. You know I'll never sub to you."

"Yeah, but you'll sub for me." Sully shot her that lopsided grin that other subs found irresistible.

"Shut up, Sully. I have no idea why you keep trying with the grin. After more than a decade, you should acknowledge I'm immune, and give up."

"True, but the optimist in me says that as long as we're both breathing, there's a chance."

Finn placed the last of the food on the table and sat in the seat to Sully's left before dishing up his own meal.

"I wouldn't call that optimism, Sully," Mac retorted, "I would call it not knowing when to quit."

"Cheeky wench. You'd miss it if I didn't shoot you the Sully grin every once in a while."

Mac's voice oozed sarcasm as she raised an eyebrow. "Okay, I admit it, my life would be devoid of meaning if I were to never again be the recipient of your knicker-dropping grin." She turned to Finn and asked, "Can you please pass the Naan?"

THREE

MAC ENJOYED the good-natured banter she shared with Sully while they ate, but once supper was done, Sully's voice turned serious.

"All right you two. It's time to work out the issues and figure a way for you to get along. We all know my part in this mess, and the toll it's taken. The way I see it we only have one issue to address. Mac needing medication to control performance anxiety, and Finn's fanatical repugnance to any kind of drug dependency."

"Hold on, Sully, I believe there are situations where medication is appropriate," Finn objected.

Mac's voice dripped with disdain. "Oh, you mean like when a guy wants to fuck, and can't get it up?"

"Mac, that's enough," Sully snapped. "Both of you, not one more word before I'm done."

With nods from both Finn and Mac, Sully continued, "Considering the situation, I am not going to maintain any confidences for either of you if I think they will help us come to an understanding. Agreed?" Sully looked at Mac and waited for her nod before turning to Finn for his.

"Mac, Finn's wife died from a heroin overdose. She suffered from panic attacks. Her doctor prescribed medication, but it wasn't long before she started self-medicating and heroin became her drug of choice."

Finn nodded at Sully and took over. "She was looking to numb out. The medication she was prescribed didn't do it for her, so she sought out drugs that would. By the time I'd clued in, she'd already worked her way up to heroin. I was so caught up in my career, I didn't notice things were so bad until it was too late. I thought I had convinced her to go to rehab, but before I could make arrangements, she'd overdosed. She was in her car when they found her body."

"Holy shit. That's awful." Mac met Finn's gaze with tears in her eyes. "I'm so sorry."

Knowing what Sully was about to reveal about herself, Mac gave him a quick glance and said, "I've got this." She turned back to Finn and, after a big shaky breath, she began.

"I didn't always suffer from performance anxiety. Well, I was always a little nervous before playing, but it was the kind of nervous that I think helped me give a little something extra that wasn't there at rehearsal."

Sully stroked Mac's forearm and encouraged her to continue. "Deep breath, sweetie. You're doing fine. Better it comes from you. The more you talk about it, the smaller it gets. I promise."

She didn't want to do this. Saying it out loud would bring it back and make it real. She much preferred to keep it safely in her back pocket where she could sit on it and squish it into something tiny and inconsequential.

Mac sucked in another big breath and let it trickle through her clenched teeth. "I had just finished my final recital and my first gruelling year of university was over. I was in a practice room putting my gear away...I didn't hear the door open, I was so far in my head. After a performance, it takes hours before I mellow out. Anyway, I had just finished zipping up my case, when I was grabbed by the hair and my face was slammed into the wall. The next thing I knew, my mouth was taped shut, and I was strapped naked to the piano bench and being told with each agonising thrust that I had no business playing a flawless recital. That it should have been his. The next thing I remember was freaking out in the ambulance. I'll let Sully tell the rest. I only know his version, anyway."

Sully continued to stroke Mac's arm. "Understanding Mac's need to decompress after a concert, I didn't go with her to pack up, but I was so pumped by her fabulous performance, I got impatient and went to look for her."

Mac listened to Sully recount the part she was missing. She both loved and hated that she couldn't remember. She loved not having more horrible memories to live with, but hated having even the smallest part of her mind stolen by the actions of another.

"I knew something was wrong when I saw the blind was down on the window of the practice room. Mac never, ever closed the blinds. I unlocked the door, and well, you know what I saw when I opened it.

"The guy was another oboist in our studio. Mac's perfect performance took him out of contention for a scholarship that provided the winner with a new instrument, tuition and living expenses for the remaining three years. Attacking Mac was how he managed his disappointment."

Mac stole a look at Finn to gauge his reaction. The tears in his eyes were her first indication that maybe he wasn't quite as big an asshole as she'd first thought.

"Anyway, I pulled him off and kneed him in the balls

with everything I had and called 911. I freed Mac and covered her with her coat. She wouldn't let me hold her or comfort her. All I could do was watch her rock in the corner. Fucking broke my heart. Every time that fucker lifted his head, I gave him another shot to the nads until the cops arrived."

Finn's voice cracked with emotion. "Christ. Mac, I just don't have words. I'm sorry doesn't even come close."

Mac sat still and stared at her empty plate as she packed up her emotional baggage and jammed it back into her pocket. She was relieved when Sully changed the subject. It was nice that he knew her so well.

"Right, how about you make Mac a nice cup of tea. She likes it a bit on the strong side with a good amount of milk."

Finn rose from his seat and started gathering dishes. "Tea, I can do. How about you, Sully?"

"What I'd really like is a good stiff drink, but I'll settle for a Coke."

"Right then, I'll be back in a jiffy," Finn said.

"Mac, sweetie?"

Mac looked up at Sully. "Yeah?"

"Oh honey, I'm so sorry. That's the last thing in the world I wanted to do, but I knew in the end it would be the kindest. I'm sure you don't think so now…"

"No, it's fine, Sully. It was a long time ago, and I should be over it."

"Yes, it was a long time ago, but no, you'll never be over it, and nobody who loves you would ever expect you to be. All we want for you is to find a way to live, really live, in spite of it. In the meantime, you have to go out there and save my ass. I love you, Mac."

"I love you too, you wanker. Now did somebody mention tea?"

Finn put the kettle on and started loading the dishwasher. Sully's sanitised version had him believing she was medicating over a few butterflies in her belly, but this was a game changer. Rape was not the land mine he thought he'd be dodging. The longer he sat through the sordid tale, the more his stomach felt like returning his supper, along with everything else he'd consumed in the last week.

He sure had a lot of shitty behaviour to make up for. Luckily, he had Sully's handy dandy list of helpful tips and suggestions. That should provide a safe starting point.

He was staring out the window into the darkness when he heard dishes being set on the counter. He turned to see Mac, looking fairly well composed, considering. "Thanks. I was just about to come and get them, but got lost in the void."

"You're welcome. Can I help with anything?"

"No, I'm almost done." Finn gestured to the table. "Mac, can we sit and talk for a minute?"

"I suppose," she said, as she sat in the chair closest to her.

Finn took the chair across from her. "I know I've been an insufferable prick at best. I'm sorry. From Sully's explanation, I pegged you as the sort of person who'd turn to chemicals over a broken nail. That's the sort of person my wife was. If she couldn't get a manicure the moment the urge struck her, she popped a pill. If she couldn't find exactly the right colour shoes to match her new dress, she popped a pill."

Mac's mouth dropped open. "You're kidding, right?"

"I wish I were. You and I have good reasons for our issues. I think I get that you and my wife are nothing alike and I'm done using her behaviour to judge you. Whether you take meds or not is none of my business, and I'll consider the matter closed. How about you?"

Mac winked. "What matter?"

Finn smiled back at her. "I'll finish cleaning up here and I'll bring your tea in when I'm done. Can you grab a Coke for Sully? "

"Sure, no problem. Thanks for making tea. And thanks for not getting weird or treating me like a freak after hearing my tale of woe."

Having no idea how best to respond, he simply said, "You're welcome."

Finn watched Mac take a Coke from the fridge and leave to sit with Sully. He packed away the leftovers and finished dealing with the kitchen. By the time the kettle had boiled, he had the beginnings of an action plan. He prepared Mac's tea then grabbed himself a Coke from the fridge on his way to the dining room.

Finn placed the steaming mug in front of Mac. "Here you go. I hope it's how you like it. Sully, why don't we go sit in the living room where I'm sure you'd be more comfortable."

"Great idea. You guys go on in, it'll take me a minute to get mobile, and while I'm already up, I may as well hit the head. I'll try not to be long, but I'm not exactly a speed demon these days."

Mac and Finn waited until Sully got to his feet before grabbing their drinks and making their way to the living room. Finn invited Mac to sit on the sofa before settling himself on the floor next to her legs. At her confused look, he said, "Sully said you love a good foot rub, and given you won't be getting any from him for a while, and you're bailing us out of a jam, and I've been such an asshole, and feel free to stop me any time..."

Mac giggled, "No, no, you're doing fine, carry on."

"Imp." He shot her a cheeky grin. "Well?"

"While I love a good foot rub, my hands are in greater need. I haven't done this much reed work in such a short time since university."

"I can do hands." Finn shifted from the floor and sat next to Mac, careful to leave what he hoped was enough space for her to be comfortable.

Sully arrived and parked himself in the chair with the best view of the action.

Finn started with Mac's left hand, working deep into the muscle at the base of her thumb before moving outward and gently rubbing each finger from palm to tip.

By the time Finn had moved on to her right hand, Mac's eyes were closed and her head settled against the back of the sofa. Every so often, she gave a small moan, each sending another shot of blood to Finn's already over-inflated penis.

"Mac, I'd quit with the moaning if I were you. I think you're restricting Finn's blood flow to his brain," Sully teased.

She lifted a foot and wiggled her toes at Sully. "Careful, or I'll let him rub my feet just to spite you. Finn, please tell me you don't have a foot fetish too."

Finn laughed. "No, your feet only need be wary of Sully the foot fondler. I just like making a woman feel good, so I'm happy to rub whatever she wants me to."

Mac blushed and Finn took pity on her. "Five more minutes, and then we have to get going."

Mac glanced at her watch. "You may need to get going, but I don't need to leave for another twenty minutes."

"Leave when I do, and you can have another hand rub before the rest of the guys arrive."

"That's okay. I'm perfectly happy with the one I got."

Finn looked to Sully for support, but only got the universal code for quit while you are behind — an index finger slicing across his throat. He nodded and gave the back of Mac's hand a gentle pat. "Right then, I have to get moving. I will see you soon, and drive carefully."

Finn rose and gave Sully's shoulder a farewell squeeze and with a pointed look said, "I'll talk to you later."

"You bet."

MAC GLOWERED at Sully

"Oh, don't look at me like that, Mac. He wasn't to know I'm the only man you'll be alone with. That is going to have to change, you know. There are men who are good, and kind, and trustworthy. Men who would treat you like you deserve to be treated. There are men out there who you can be alone with and be safe. Men you can even have sex with. Honey, it's time to push your boundaries, and I think Finn might be the guy to do it with."

"I want my quiet life back, Sully. It was quiet up until yesterday." Mac knew he was right, but that didn't change how she felt.

"Sometimes, we can't go back. Come on, Mac, you know he gets your motor going. I thought you were going to come right there in that chair just from that hand massage."

"I will concede that I may have felt a wee tingle in parts that have been tingle-less for a number of years."

"I knew it."

"Oh, don't go getting all smug on me. I have a perfectly good Rabbit to take care of that annoying little tingle."

"It'll do for now, sweetie."

"I've got to get moving too. What can I do for you before I go?"

"I think I'll be fine, kiddo. Once you're on your way, I'll just settle myself in bed with a nice pain pill, a can of Coke, and my remote control."

"Okay, if you're sure."

"I'm good. You don't want to be late."

"I won't be. You head off to bed. I'll just set some reeds to soak and lock up when I leave."

"Alright. G'night, sweetheart."

"G'night, Sully."

FINN FLOPPED into his favourite armchair as he held the phone to his ear. "Hi, it's about time you called."

"Sorry. Mac only just left. I know she was holding off until the last possible minute."

"And why is that exactly, Sully?" Finn asked.

"Yeah, I knew this is why you wanted me to call. I wish we'd got it all out of the way tonight, but you have to agree, she'd had more than enough, especially this close to a performance."

Finn thought back to the determined look on Mac's face when Sully was done telling the story, and realised she'd been at her limit. "Good grief, just get on with it before she gets here."

"She can't be alone with a man. I'm the only one she feels safe with."

"Well that explains the look in her eyes when the guys all left last night."

"We're going to have to work on it. I've let it go far too long. In the meantime, make sure she's never left alone, okay?"

"Got it. That fucker really did a number on her. Please tell me he got all that was coming to him."

Sully gave a heavy sigh. "He got fourteen years, but only has to serve just over nine. That means he gets out next year. It took almost two years from laying charges to sentencing. He was denied bail for all that time, and at sentencing, the judge refused to give him any credit for time served. Otherwise, he'd have been out already"

The ball of anger in Finn's stomach grew with each new detail about Mac's attack and its repercussions. "Not enough, but at least he got jail-time. I guess getting caught in the act would go a long way to a conviction."

"Yeah. You'd think the dumb fuck would have pleaded guilty, but he fought to the bitter end. I don't think that won him any points with the judge."

"Okay, so is there anything else I should know?"

"I think that's it, except maybe just let the beta-blocker issue go. At least until she's done subbing for me."

"I already did. Mac and I had that conversation in the kitchen when she brought in the dishes. I would like to find a way to help her so she doesn't need them to perform, but after tonight's horrifying revelations, I will hold off. Now about the play party on Sunday. I know you won't be playing, but do you think there's any chance you could get Mac to come?"

"I'll see what I can do. I've been known to play the guilt card on occasion. This might be an appropriate time."

"Didn't you use it to get her to play for you?"

"Nope. That was an act of love, pure and simple. The guilt card is only required if I ask something truly decadent of her."

"Gotta go, that's the door. I'll catch you later."

"G'night."

Mac stroked Gounod on her lap as she waited for Sully to answer his phone.

"Hey, how did it go tonight, sweetie?"

"Really well. I didn't even need to take a beta blocker."

"That's awesome. I knew you'd be fine."

"I know that won't be the case tomorrow night, though."

"That's okay, do what you can. Finn gets it. He won't be on your case about it any more, but that doesn't mean he won't work at finding another way to deal."

"Yeah, I know. We talked about it earlier. It was hard to believe he was the same person I met last night. He went from total asshole to sweet and thoughtful. It almost gave me whiplash."

"I told you he really wasn't an asshole. What happened with his wife warped his view of anxiety and medication."

"Yeah, I get it. At least we're able to have a functional working relationship."

"That's a start. So, Finn's got a play party coming up on Sunday. I won't be able to play, but I'm going to attend anyway. How about you join me."

Mac's answer was instant. "No."

"Aw, come on, Mac. It'll be fun. You don't have to play. Just keep me company."

"Fuck you, Sully. You aren't being fair. I know when you're inching towards a guilt trip. It's not going to work this time."

"It's not some random party, Mac. It's restricted to the quintet members and their subs. There's no pressure. It's just a social occasion where we get to let off steam. You aren't the only one who needs to decompress after performing. When we have a crazy concert schedule, like we do every December, Finn throws end of week play parties."

"No. I am not part of the quintet, and I am not anyone's sub."

"Right now you are part of the quintet, and while you may not belong to anyone, you are a sub."

"Fuck. Why are you pushing this? I agreed to perform a bunch of concerts in your place. That was all we'd agreed to. You never said anything about play parties, or any other social activities."

"True, I didn't include socialising in my request, but I'm asking now. I want to go to the party, and if I don't get to play, I'd like to have someone to keep me company."

Mac was torn. She'd spent years avoiding social situations. She felt safer and more in control that way, but sometimes she missed letting loose and having some fun with a group of people.

"I wouldn't be expected to play?"

"Not if you don't want to. You know the way it works. Nothing's changed. Safe, Sane, and Consensual. You know I'd cut off my lips and rip my own lungs out before I'd ever put you at risk."

"Yeah, but would you play a concert on a commercial reed?"

"In a heartbeat. So, will ya, will ya?"

Mac could feel herself being swayed. Sully had protected her for years. Her head knew he would never put her safety at risk, but that didn't stop her from being afraid.

"I don't know. It's been so long since I've been to any party, let alone a kinky one."

I know, sweetheart. Just give it a try. If it's too much for you, we'll leave. Who knows, you might just have a little fun for a change.

"I hate you, Sully. I really, really hate you."

"No you don't. You love me to pieces. You can pick me up at seven."

"Fine. G'night."

"Good night, sweetheart."

Miserable fucker. Yet another thing he'd talked her into. How much more upheaval would he wreak upon her before his ribs healed. Oh well, she'd had a pretty good rehearsal, and getting through without needing a blocker made it that much better. That hand rub sure helped mitigate the earlier unpleasantness of the evening, and now she and Finn were no longer at odds with each other, she hoped things would go smoothly until her obligation to Sully and his quintet was over.

FOUR

Mac was bombarded by the other members of the quintet the moment they left the stage.

"Great concert, Mac," Griff said, as he gave her a pat on the shoulder.

"Yeah, I thought I'd seen your A game, but, wow." Jack added.

"Thanks, guys. I think we all kicked-ass tonight and I'm glad I didn't let you down."

"You were completely fab. Wanna join us at the pub for a drink to wind down?" Wilson asked.

"I appreciate the offer, but I need to head home. I decompress better there."

"Okay, but we'll be at the Squeaky Wheel if you change your mind."

Mac donned her coat and grabbed her gear as she headed for her car. "Good night. I'll see you all tomorrow night."

The men waved to Mac as she left. Finn opened the door for her, watching until he she'd made it safely to her vehicle and was driving away. He appreciated that she checked the inside of her car carefully before opening the door and getting in. He would have preferred to walk her to her car, but based on what Sully'd told him, he figured she wouldn't be good with that, and he didn't want to put her on the spot by asking.

Baby steps. She rehearsed the night before without meds. That was huge to him. She'd agreed to come to the play party with Sully. That was huge in a whole other way. Well, off to the pub to drink with the boys. He'd have to give them some background on Mac so they could be aware of possible triggers. Why did he always have to fall for the damaged ones? At least with Mac, her anxiety was strictly limited to performance situations. As long as it stayed that way, he would deal.

MAC'S PHONE started ringing just as she settled into bed with a steaming cup of tea. She knew who it would be, even before looking at the caller ID.

"Hi, Sully."

"Hey gorgeous, great gig tonight. I don't think I've ever heard you sound better."

"You were there?"

"Of course I was there. Your first performance in years? I'd have to be crossing the threshold of death's door to miss that."

"Thanks for being there. You should have told me you were coming."

"Nope, you had enough on your mind. I didn't want to risk being any kind of distraction for you. Anyway, I know you have a post-performance ritual, so I will let you get back to it. I just wanted to let you know how awesome you were and how proud of you I am."

"Thanks. Sometimes, I think you know me way too well, but I'm really glad you do."

"Goodnight, sweetheart."

"Goodnight."

Mac sipped her tea as she considered her best friend. He would make someone very lucky one day. Too bad he didn't have a nice, regular woman to be taking care of him while he's out of commission. On second thought, it's probably just as well. His rampant libido and non-existent self control would likely hold back his recovery. Hell, that's what got his ribs broken in the first place. At least he wouldn't get a chance to over-do it at the play party. That was probably the only good thing she could come up with about letting Sully talk her into going.

Bugger. It had been so long since she'd been around any of that kind of activity in real life. She had been just getting involved when her world imploded. While her interest remained, she limited her indulgence to online lurking. She and Sully talked about it, but mostly in the context of his exploits.

While she often masturbated to Sully's anecdotes, it was only the sub's experience that turned her on. Because theirs was a sibling-like relationship, she consciously replaced Sully with the Dom of her dreams. Somehow over the last few days, the Dom of her dreams had morphed into Finn.

Finn. How on earth was she going to handle watching him play with someone else? True, the only playing she'd done in years happened in her head, and the prospect of a physical experience was too terrifying to contemplate. Of course, she didn't have to watch Finn. The rest of the quintet would be there. She could watch them. Besides, she was only going to keep Sully from feeling like a wallflower. Maybe just being there, watching the action live, would help her shift from fantasy-land to reality.

FIVE

MAC FIDGETED as she and Sully waited at Finn's front door. "It'll be fine. I'll be there the whole time, but if I do have to leave you for any reason, you know, like taking a piss, I'll make sure you are safe and not left alone. Trust me."

"I do trust you. You know I do. That doesn't make this any less scary, though."

"It's okay to be scared as long as it doesn't hold you back. You've been letting it hold you back for too long."

Their conversation stopped as they heard the lock being released, and they both turned to face the door.

Finn appeared and smiled. "Great, you both made it. Come on in, we're just getting organised. Now that you're here, we can get started."

Mac and Sully entered and stowed their outerwear. Finn continued as he locked the door behind them, "I've set up seating for you in the after-care area, which should afford you both a good view of most, if not all the action. There is a refreshment table there as well, so please, do help yourselves."

They made their way through to the kitchen, where an open door revealed a staircase to the basement.

"Hold onto the banister and watch your step. It's a little steep. We can't afford another injured oboist."

At the bottom of the stairs, Mac got her first glimpse of the playroom. It was post and beam and seemed to span almost the entire footprint of the house. Her first instinct was to turn tail and run, but curiosity and her commitment to Sully won out. That, and Sully prodding her along from behind.

She spotted the after-care area in the far corner and they skirted the perimeter of the room to get there without disturbing those who were already playing.

"You're a real joker. A fainting couch? Fuck, Finn, why don't you just lop off my balls right now," Sully complained.

"Oh, suck it up, buttercup. It was the most comfortable option I could think of. I could go get you a ladder-back chair from the kitchen if you would prefer, because that nice comfy chair next to the couch is for Mac."

Mac smirked at the exchange and felt her shoulders relax a bit.

"Have a seat while our diva decides whether he requires an uncomfortable chair to prove his manliness." Finn indicated a recliner to Mac that would have suited Sully's needs perfectly, and feeling a touch mischievous, she accepted.

Sully huffed. "Fuck you, Finn. And you too, Mac."

Mac rolled her eyes at Finn and giggled. He responded with a wink, sparking that increasingly familiar tingle between her legs.

"Oh, settle yourself down before you disturb a scene." Finn reached for a Coke and waited for Sully to get himself comfortable before handing it over. "Can I get you something, Mac?"

"I'm fine for now, thanks."

Mac gave a little jump when she felt Finn settle on the floor and take her right foot in his hands. "What on earth are you doing? You should be attending to your sub, not fulfilling Sully's foot fantasies."

"And if I had a sub here, I would be attending to her needs. Since I don't, I am free to attend to yours. Now just sit back, watch whatever scenes interest you, and enjoy."

FINN KEPT a close eye on which scenes grabbed Mac's attention and filed them away for future reference. The activities she watched openly would be good rewards for her trying the ones she was uncomfortable about, yet found irresistible. He continued to rub her feet, but occasionally worked his way up to her calves, careful not to overstay his welcome.

The way Mac's eyes kept wandering to the corner of the room where Jackson sat in a chair, spanking the sub draped over his lap, gave Finn his first clue to what Mac found appealing. If it hadn't been for her slight shiver and the small, sharp intake of breath, he would have missed her quick glance at Wilson working his rope magic. Interesting. Something to keep in mind for the very distant future, if ever. He knew what seemed arousing in fantasy, could be disastrous in reality, and with Mac's experience, he didn't feel particularly optimistic on that front. While he liked to work with rope occasionally, it didn't get him all fired up like it did Wilson.

Mac interrupted his thoughts. "Finn, you can stop any time."

"I told you I would be attending your needs today, and unless there is something you need more than your feet rubbed, I'm happy to keep doing what I'm doing. Is there something more pressing you need?"

"Um, no. It's just that you've been at it for an awfully long time, and while it feels great, I don't want to monopolise you."

"We'll just carry on then, shall we?"

"Yeah, I guess."

EVEN THOUGH EVERYONE else was leaving, Mac didn't want to go. She was completely relaxed, and one look at Sully told her he was perfectly happy to stay put. To hell with it. She wanted to spend more time with Finn and with Sully here, she was safe.

She looked up and smiled as Finn returned to the play-room after seeing the last of his guests out the door.

"Mmm, there's nothing I like better than a contented smile, especially if I helped produce it."

"Stop fishing. Yes, you're the main cause, but don't let it go to your head."

"I'll try not to. It's getting late, and Sully is looking rather comfortable. How about you both spend the night?"

Mac sucked in a breath and let it out slowly as she tried to control her panic. "Absolutely not. Sully can stay. I'll pick him up in the morning and take him home."

Sully piped up. "Oh, Mac, come on, it's just a sleepover. You can even bring me breakfast in bed. It'll be fun. You may not think so right now because it's outside of your comfort-zone, but honey, you've gotta start pushing the boundaries, and with me here, and Finn knowing the whole score, it's probably the safest opportunity you could ask for."

"I can't believe you think the prospect of me bringing you breakfast in bed qualifies as incentive. I already moved out of my comfort-zone by attending this party. Don't you think that's enough for one day?"

"I know how hard it was for you to come tonight. But you are so strong, and so capable of pushing harder than this, and I think you should. You know about safewords. Stay a little longer, and see how you feel. If you're uncomfortable, just say yellow, and we'll do whatever is necessary to get you back to green, and if you really need to bail, just call red. Okay?"

"I don't know, Sully. I'm scared."

"I know, sweetheart. We talked about this. I want you to think very carefully, will giving in to your fear be holding you back?"

Mac waffled back and forth, but in her heart, she knew Sully was right. She was letting fear hold her back. She hated when Sully was right. It made him rather insufferable as he rubbed it in. Fuck it. Every time she let her fear rule her, that monster won. Maybe it was time to start taking back her life. "If I were to stay, where would I sleep?"

Finn spoke up. "I have a couple of spare rooms. I promise, absolutely nothing will happen you don't want to happen. Okay? Like Sully said, you have safewords, and they work for every situation, no matter what."

Mac hugged her knees, and rested her chin on top of them. She closed her eyes, took in a long, deep breath, held it, and waited for her heart to stop hammering before she let it escape. "Okay, I'll try."

"Good," Sully said, "now can we move this party

upstairs? As comfy as this damned fainting couch is, I don't want to end up sleeping on it."

So far, so good, Finn thought as he followed Sully and Mac up the stairs. He and Sully figured they'd be doing well if they got Mac to stay until everyone else had left the play party. That she had agreed to spend the night, was beyond a bonus. Of course agreeing to spend the night, and actually doing it, were two completely different things. "Sully, how about you come with me to show Mac to her room before you head on to yours."

"We're going to bed now?" Mac asked.

Finn couldn't help but feel a little triumphant at the disappointment he saw on Mac's face. So far, the night had been a total success, and he was not going to do anything to jeopardise it. "Yes, we're going to bed now. One look, and I can tell you're both shattered. A good night's sleep is what we all need, so let's get a move on."

SIX

THE SCREAM that jolted him from sleep had already stopped, but the muffled moans had him out of bed and through the door before his brain had really kicked in. "What the fuck?" It was fortunate he'd chosen to wear pyjama bottoms to bed, because he was already in Mac's room before his choice of sleepwear became a consideration. He raced to the bed and crouched next to it as he flipped on the lamp. He remained perfectly still and spoke softly. "Mac, wake up, love. It's just a bad dream. I'm not going to touch you, but you need to wake up, baby."

Mac continued to moan, and Finn let out a sigh of relief as he heard Sully come shuffling through the door. "Thank fuck. Get in here and do something. I don't want to touch her and freak her out more, but she's not responding to my words."

"Dammit, I thought she was over this. I'll talk to her, but you're going to have to hold her, because she might struggle, even with me. Just try and hold her so she'll see me when she opens her eyes."

Finn eased onto the bed beside Mac. As he slipped his

arms around her and gently pulled her into his side, she went limp and stopped moaning. He rocked her gently as he stroked her hand and rubbed his cheek against the top of her head.

"Mac, wake up, sweetie. Finn's got you." Sully stroked her cheek and tried again. "Come on, Mac. You need to wake up. Finn's got you, but you're safe. I promise, you're safe."

Finn knew the instant she woke up. Her body stiffened for a moment before the struggling began.

"Enough," Finn ordered. Mac obeyed and Finn continued, "Mac, you're fine love. You were having a nightmare, and just talking to you wasn't helping. Give me a colour."

After a brief pause, Mac replied, "Yellow."

"Yellow we can work with. Does something need to change, or do you just need a minute."

Mac took a little longer, then relaxed back into Finn's side as she said, "I just need a minute."

Sully stroked Mac's cheek once more and asked, "Do you need me to stay, or are you okay with me heading back to my own bed?"

Mac turned her head and looked into Finn's eyes before answering. "I think I'll be okay, you go back to bed."

"Brave girl. I'll see you in the morning."

Finn shifted their bodies so he was sitting against the headboard with Mac's body snuggled tight to his side, her legs draped over his lap.

They sat like that for a long time before Mac finally spoke. "Finn?"

"Yeah?"

"Thank you."

"What for?"

"Not being the asshole I first thought you were for starters, I think."

Finn chuckled. "Thank you for not being the junkie I first took you for."

"What a pair we are."

"Well, now that we know what we aren't, how about we get a better idea of what we are?"

"Okay, you go first."

"Remember, you can still use your safewords at any time."

"I'll remember."

Finn thought hard. Talk about walking a fine line. What to ask that pushes the envelope without tearing it? He needed to make this question count because he didn't want to make her shut down. "Right then, let's go for an easy one. What's your favourite part of a man's body. Where do your eyes go first when you meet a man you find interesting?"

"I check out the upper arms. I like them to be muscular, but not in a body-builder way. If a guy needs to flex his biceps in the mirror, his arms are too muscular. I want to feel like those arms are for holding me and keeping me safe, not for his own personal eye-candy."

Finn chuckled. "I can assure you that I never flex any of my muscles in a mirror. I'm going to cheat a bit, and ask a follow up question. How would you rate my arms?"

He resisted the groan that threatened when Mac reached up and gave his left biceps a bit of a squeeze.

"I'd say you're well within acceptable muscular parameters."

"That's a relief. Your turn to ask me something."

"Same question."

"My favourite part on a man's body is..."

Mac giggled. "Smart-ass. You know what I meant."

Finn toyed with giving a less provocative answer, but he

refused to be anything less than completely honest. "Okay, I'd have to say lips. They're so very versatile."

"I buy that."

Finn watched with interest as Mac caught her lower lip in her teeth and screwed her eyes shut. He waited patiently for her to resolve her inner conflict.

With her eyes still squeezed shut, she said, "You got a follow up, so it's only fair that I do too. How would you rate my lips?" She'd no sooner got the words out and her face was buried into his shoulder.

Finn just about stopped breathing. It was the logical follow up, but that she'd asked it had him scrambling for a satisfactory answer that wouldn't scare the shit out of her. Finally, he went with his instincts.

He took her chin between his thumb and forefinger, then gently guided her face to meet his. He paused for a moment and looked into her eyes before touching his lips to hers. "Kissable, most definitely kissable," he declared. He gave her another, slightly longer kiss before releasing her chin. Finn was worried he'd pushed too far, but it was too to late change it.

Mac sighed. "That's a relief."

Finn hugged Mac a little closer to him and kissed the top of her head. "Are you up for another question, or are you ready to go back to sleep?"

"I'm feeling pretty sleepy."

"Alright. Let's get you all tucked in before I head back to bed, then."

Mac stiffened, then asked, "Can you stay with me? At least until I fall asleep?"

"Whatever you need."

Finn extricated himself from Mac and waited for her to settle back into bed. Sensing she needed him to do more than sit on the edge of the bed and hold her hand until she fell asleep, he eased in, then tucked her into his side with her head resting on his chest. "This okay?"

Finn felt her nod. He waited a few extra minutes after her body went slack to be sure she was asleep before trying to disengage himself from their tangled bodies. He wanted to stay, but didn't want to do anything that might snuff out that tiny glimmer of trust she was developing in him.

SOMETHING WAS WRONG. Mac clawed her way from sleep as she realised Finn was getting out of bed. She'd felt safe and content in his arms. Panic gripped her, and she said the first thing that came to mind. "Yellow."

"What?"

"Yellow."

"Okay. Does something need to change, or do you just need a minute?"

"That depends."

"You're going to have to give me more than that, baby."

"It depends on whether you're leaving or just shifting position."

Please don't leave me. She was surprised by her silent plea. Sully had slept with her and kept her safe for months after it happened, but never once, did she feel content.

Finn stroked her cheek. "I promised to stay until you fell asleep. I thought you had, so I was heading back to my own bed. Now, what do you need, so we can fix it?

Mac paused, squeezing her hands in and out of fists before she gathered the courage to respond. "I need you to stay."

"Brave girl. That was a pretty scary thing to say, wasn't it?"

"Yeah."

"Here's the deal, Mac. The last thing I want to do right now is leave. So I need to be absolutely clear about what you are asking. There can be no room for interpretation. Are you asking me to sleep in this bed, snuggled up with you for the rest of the night?"

Mac's heart was beating nineteen to the dozen, but she wanted him to stay more than she was scared. "Yes, I want you to sleep with me cuddled safe in your arms for the rest of the night."

"I can do that, my sweet, brave girl."

As Finn settled in next to Mac, she instantly burrowed into his side and relaxed. Moments later, as she was drifting back to sleep, she wished Finn had kissed her good night.

THE FIRST RAYS of morning were trickling through the blinds and Finn lay on his side watching Mac as she slept. He recalled the two kisses they'd shared the previous night along with her murmured wish, and cursed the thought as he inched his pelvis away to keep his inconvenient erection from scaring her. He was already concerned about how she'd react to waking up with him in her bed.

Would it be best to sneak out of bed and let her wake up alone or not? He teetered back and forth a number of times before not won. Selfish bastard that he was, he couldn't bear to leave her before he absolutely had to.

He knew he should let her sleep until she was ready to wake up on her own, but his usual intractable self-control was distinctly absent. That happened a lot when it came to Mac.

He wet his index finger and traced it around Mac's lips. Her eyelids flickered and then opened. There was a moment of confusion in her eyes before she smiled wide and said, "You stayed."

"I told you I would. I'm sorry to wake you, but I

wanted to give you the goodnight kiss you asked for last night, and I couldn't wait any longer."

"I remember thinking it, but I don't remember saying it out loud. And if you did hear me ask, why didn't you do it last night?

"You were mumbling and not fully awake. I would have loved to kiss you goodnight then, but I wanted you to be awake enough to enjoy it with me."

"You didn't want to freak me out when I was half a sleep."

"That too. So, can I kiss you goodnight now?"

Mac nodded, and Finn said, "I need to hear the words, Mac. I know it's hard, but I'm not willing to risk fucking up whatever we might have, on miscommunication."

"Fair enough. May I have my goodnight kiss now?"

Finn answered with his lips barely touching hers. A whisper that increased in volume as Mac's lips parted to allow his teasing tongue entry.

Finn eased back and gazed into Mac's eyes. "Goodnight, Mac." After a short pause, he said, "May I kiss you good morning?"

Mac responded with an enthusiastic, "Yes, please."

Finn demanded more with this kiss, and Mac opened to him without hesitation. He wanted to lose himself in her mouth and kiss her for days. He shifted gears, and gentled the kiss before he reluctantly pulled away. He returned his gaze to hers and grinned. "Wow, that was some kiss good morning."

"A girl could get used to spending the night with a man if the morning promises kisses like that."

Finn knew he was falling harder with each passing day, and it scared him more than he wanted to admit. Especially to himself. "Alright, greedy-lips. It's time to get moving. We have an invalid in the next room who's probably wide awake and wondering why he's still waiting for his breakfast in bed."

"Hell, I think you just may know Sully almost as well as I do."

"Quite possibly. I'm going to go check on him and put some clothes on. I'll meet you in the kitchen."

"You do know I can't cook, right?"

"I'm sure you can manage to throw some slices of bread in a toaster and slather them in coronary-inducing quantities of butter."

"Yeah, I can just about manage that."

FINN POKED his head through the doorway and wasn't surprised to find Sully awake and full of questions.

"It was mighty quiet after I returned to my very lonely bed last night. No screaming from nightmares or mind-blowing orgasms. And where's my breakfast?"

"Good morning to you too, you cheeky fuck."

"Tell me what happened after I left. You know how I hate being left out of the know."

"We asked each other a getting to know you question. She gave my biceps a squeeze, I gave her lips a smooch, I spent the night snuggled up with her, and now it's morning."

"I suspect you've omitted a few details, but that's okay, I'll press Mac for them later." Sully cocked his head. "Seriously, she was okay last night and this morning?"

"Yeah. Actually, she was way better than I had any right to hope she'd be. I really like her, and I don't want to fuck up."

"You're doing fine. I should have started urging her to break free of her self-imposed exile years ago, but it was too easy to let her hide from the world, and lean on me. It broke my heart to watch her world shrink to nothing but her cat and me, but I was too scared to give her some tough love in case she shut me out too.

"At least now, it looks like she's finally ready to take back her life, and I think you're the guy to help her do it. If it weren't for my damn foot fetish, I'm sure she'd be all over me. But, c'est la vie."

"Sorry, pal, I think your foot-fetish is just her excuse to let you down gently. I was thinking about Christmas. Does she spend it with family?"

"No. Every year I try to get her to come and spend it with me at my parents' house, and every year she turns me down flat. She spends it by herself and she insists that's how she likes it. Maybe this year will be different."

"Maybe. I'd best get downstairs and get your breakfast started. I lit a fire under Mac's ass to meet me in the kitchen, and I doubt she'll thrilled if I make her wait. She insists she can't cook."

"And, she'd be right. I'm not kidding when I say, no matter what, do not let her cook."

"I've put her on toast duty. Please tell me that's safe."

"That's about the only thing that is safe, provided you have the toaster settings to barely tanned."

"Good to know. I'll see you in a bit with breakfast and coffee."

FINN WATCHED Mac struggle with the coffee maker for a few minutes before taking pity on her. "I'll do that, you go sit down."

"What took you so long? I told you I can't cook."

"Sully was being nosy. I didn't realise your inability to cook extended to use of a coffee maker.

"I drink tea, so I only needed to master a kettle. I assume, given how long you were with him, his Lordship had the blow by blow of last night. I can't believe men accuse women of being gossip-mongers."

Finn let out a rumbling laugh. "While he has been provided with a brief overview, he plans to grill you for the details. As for blow by blow, I'm quite certain I would have noticed, and remembered had blowing been involved." He gave Mac an exaggerated wink and said, "I can only hope there will be some in my future."

"You never know what the future holds, do you? If, when I woke up yesterday, someone had said I would spend the night in bed with any man, let alone you, I would have laughed myself sick."

Mac's unguarded response was delightful. So much for the erection he'd wrangled into submission not ten minutes earlier. "I think we need to change the subject."

"Okay, I can blow it off if you can."

"You did that on purpose, imp."

"Didn't you have some bread you wanted me to toast and butter?"

Finn gathered the bread and butter and set it on the counter in front of the toaster. "There you go. I figure four slices for me, another four for Sully, and however many you'll eat should do it."

"On it."

"How do you like your bacon and eggs?"

"I like my bacon completely crispy and my eggs over-easy."

Finn leaned down and gave her a peck on the nose. "A woman after my own heart. There's nothing like the full cholesterol meal deal to get a good start on the day."

The smile she gave him melted him to his toes. Oh boy, was he in trouble.

"I come bearing breakfast, you lazy-ass pecker-head." Mac sauntered into Sully's room and waited for him to raise himself up before setting the bed-tray over his legs.

"Well good morning to you, my little ray of sunshine. Did you sleep well?"

"You can stop right now. Whatever Finn told you when you pumped him for information is all you're going to get, you nosy git."

"I'll take that as a yes." He grinned at her and she stuck her tongue out at him.

"You're awfully lucky I love you, you know."

"I do know. You like him, don't you?"

Sometimes she wondered if Sully could read minds because he had an eerie way of knowing what was going on in her head. "So many parts of me don't want to for so many different reasons, but yeah, I like him. It's like driving downhill in the snow. Unless I want to crash, I can only go forward, moving ever faster, and there's no way to reverse out of it."

"Then stop trying to put it in reverse. As long as there are no sharp bends in the road ahead, just sit back and enjoy the ride."

"I hate you."

"I know. Where's your breakfast?"

"Finn's bringing ours up as soon as it's ready. We figured with you being the big baby you are, we should get yours done and served first."

"I'm not a baby. I'm a finely tuned instrument that's been banged up and is in for repair."

"Whatever you need to believe, Sully."

"You are such a cheeky wench. I don't know why I put up with you."

"I let you rub my feet."

"Yeah, there is that."

FINN LOOKED up as Mac brought Sully's breakfast tray into the kitchen. "Thanks Mac, if you leave it on the counter, I'll take care of it."

She put the tray down. "I don't mind loading the dishwasher, unless you're obsessive compulsive and will reload it to your exacting specifications the moment my back's turned."

"No, I'm not that bad. If you really want to load the dishes, I'd be a fool to say no."

Finn stopped wiping down the stove for a moment and enjoyed the view of her ass as she bent to put the plates on the bottom rack. Perfect position for a nice spanking. He turned away and returned to his task. Plenty of time to fantasise later.

When he'd finished wiping all the surfaces, Finn crossed the floor and stood next to Mac. "Thanks for your help, love."

"You're welcome. Thank you for cooking breakfast. It was really good."

"Anytime." Finn's eyes focused on Mac's lips, and he had to ask. "Can I kiss you?"

Mac nodded and tilted her head up. Finn leaned down, cupping her cheek as he placed a firm kiss on her lips. He chose not to deepen it. His lips had already written cheques his dick wouldn't be cashing anytime soon.

He eased away. The sound of a voice clearing in the doorway changed his mind about dipping in for another.

"I do hope I'm not interrupting."

Finn glowered at Sully. "Fuck you. What are you doing up?"

Sully's cheeky smile lit the room. "I've had my breakfast in bed, and now I'm ready to start my day. If I let this wee wench sub for me too long, you guys'll toss my ass aside and give her my chair."

"You know damn well your chair is perfectly safe," Mac retorted.

"My chair may be, but sweetie, you are still the most amazing oboist I know, and I can't think of a bigger, badder, in your face, fuck you and the horse you rode in on to that mother-fucking piece of shit, than to go pro.

Mac collapsed onto the nearest chair. "We've talked this to death. Not going to happen. I'm perfectly happy playing just for me."

"We'll revisit this when I have working ribs and you've finished an entire Christmas concert schedule."

"Let's not and say we did."

"I'm going to let this drop for now, but it will come up again. Count on it. Now, I'm going to gather my bits and pieces and call a cab."

"I already told you I would drive you home, and besides, poor Gounod's been home alone all night."

"He's a fucking cat. As long as he has food, water, and a place to bury his shit, he's good."

"You can't hold a grudge just because he peed in your shoes once when he was a kitten."

"I can, and do."

Fine, but I'm still driving you home. Go get your shit together and I'll meet you in the living room."

Sully shuffled off, and Finn spoke up. "I'm going to ask

you something, and I want you to think about it very care-fully before you answer."

"Okay?"

"Do you think you could ever feel comfortable being alone with me?"

"I don't have to think about that. I was alone with you all night."

"Not really, Sully was in the next room."

"He may have been in the next room, but you know as well as I do, he'd have been the next best thing to useless if I'd really needed him."

"Fair enough. In that case, would you like to come over for dinner and a movie tonight? Remember, you always have your safewords, and they work for everything."

"Oh, what the hell. Go big, or go home, right? A few kisses after more than a decade without makes a girl feel a little reckless. What time shall I be here?"

"How about six?"

"Sounds good to me."

MAC HADN'T EVEN GOT her seatbelt on before Sully began his inquisition. "So, what did you two talk about in the kitchen before we left?"

Mac growled as she started the car. "None of your business, you nosy bugger."

"True, but humour me."

Before driving off, Mac turned to face Sully. "Alright, given you're my safe-call, but God help me if I need you. I'm going back tonight for dinner and a film."

"Go you." Sully patted her on the leg. "I mean that, Mac. I'm not being funny. I am so, so happy you've finally found someone you feel safe to be alone with. You deserve that. He's a good man. I've known him a long time and I've seen how he plays. And before you say a word, I know damn well he won't even think about playing with you until he knows, not sure, not confident, but knows it's what you want. I trust him to take good care of you. You have to promise me two things. One, before making any rash decisions you will come to me if you are even the tiniest bit unsure about anything. And two, you will communicate clearly with Finn. Can you promise me those two things?"

Mac considered for a moment. "I promise. You're the only man in the world, for now anyway, who I trust absolutely. If you tell me he has your trust, then I will give him the opportunity to earn mine."

"Good enough. Jeezus, woman, are you purposely picking the bumpiest route home and aiming for every single pothole along the way?"

"Sorry, bud. Road bumpiness increases exponentially to the degree of pain you're experiencing. We'll be home soon, then you can have some pain meds and go to bed with a Coke and your remote control."

"I expect you to call tomorrow with a full report on the evening's shenanigans."

"Of course you do. I'll call, and I may take pity on your poor sorry ass and provide you with a vignette of the evening, but don't count on it. Part of my decision may depend on how much more complaining you do between now and when I get you tucked into bed."

EIGHT

Finn smiled wide as he opened the door to Mac. Welcome back. It's been a pretty lonely day. How was Gounod when you got home?"

"Oh My God! You'd think I'd taken the vacuum to him followed by a thorough dunking in ice-water. He yelled at me for hours. Hours. I shit you not. Even after I gave in and opened a tin of tuna, he continued to tell me off. Who knew a cat could yell with his mouth full?"

"Poor kitty."

"Poor kitty? I'm surprised my ears aren't bleeding."

"Would a kiss help."

"It couldn't hurt."

Finn wrapped his arms around Mac and lifted her from the floor before he caressed her lips with his own. "Better?"

"Not sure. Maybe you should do that again."

He did, and her moan was all the encouragement he needed. He deepened the kiss and in one smooth motion, he had her in his arms, bridal fashion. He carried her to the sofa and sat with her in his lap. He slowly broke the kiss and looked into Mac's eyes. "Better now?"

Mac sighed. "Definitely."

"Good. Are you hungry?"

"I could eat."

"Sully said you like lasagne. I made it myself. No oven-ready abominations from the supermarket for me."

"I love lasagne. And home-made? That's a real treat."

"What I want to do, is sit here and kiss you silly, but it might be better to do that without the risk of being interrupted by growling bellies. Up you get." Finn released his grip, and Mac slid off his lap and started towards the kitchen.

"Oh no you don't. Dining room, you."

"You don't want any help?"

"Not this time. For now, just let me dote on you."

"I'm not comfortable with being doted on. I've been taking care of myself for a long time."

"We'll work on that. Off with you. I'll be through in a minute."

MAC LAID her knife and fork on her empty plate and groaned. "That was fabulous. I really shouldn't have eaten that much, but I can't remember the last time I had truly home-made lasagne. And no, restaurant lasagne doesn't qualify, no matter how authentic the claim."

"Thank you. I'm glad you enjoyed it. I do love a woman that eats."

"I like food too much to be one of those women who orders a salad and only eats half a cherry tomato and a lettuce leaf for fear she'll get fat and no man will want her.

Fuck that for a lark. Either you like me for who I am, or move on."

"I like you very much for who you are."

Mac blushed. "Aw crap, I wasn't fishing, you know."

"I know. Just putting it out there so you don't need to wonder."

"Well, so you don't need to wonder either, I like you for who you are too."

Finn smiled wide. "Ready for our movie?"

"Nope, we have a table to clear and a kitchen to clean first."

"What if I told you I'd take care of it later?"

"I'd tell you we should both deal with it now. It will take less time, be easier to clean, and it won't be lurking, waiting to pounce when you'd rather be doing something else."

"You're right, but I told you I would be doting on you."

"You can resume your dotage after."

"Alright, let's get this done, so we can snuggle and watch a film."

"What if we were to skip the film and just snuggle?"

"I'd be good with that. I'm curious about why, though."

"I need this to be real, and if we watch a film, it's too easy for me to check out."

"Are you sure this is what you want?"

"Not really, but I want to try. It wouldn't really be any different than last night, except we'd both be awake."

"Let's get a move on."

"How're you doing, Mac?"

They'd been cuddling in silence on the sofa for a good half hour before Finn spoke up.

"Okay, I think. It's scary, but not. The idea of it is scary, but it feels way more good than it does scary." Mac wasn't ready to admit out loud that the good was feeling safe and content in Finn's arms. Out loud made it real, and this was all way too new for her to let it be real yet.

"That's what I like to hear. Are you up for a little exploring?"

"Depends. What kind of exploring?"

"Mostly talking, but there'll be a little touching. Your safewords are still in play and work for everything. Okay?"

Butterflies attacked her stomach with a vengeance and she had to concentrate on not letting them take over. "I think so. What kind of talking, and what kind of touching?"

"I want to talk to you about boundaries, limits, wants, and needs. As for touching, I can't touch you anywhere or in any way that is sexual, but you can touch me anywhere and any way you want, and I'll keep my hands at my sides."

"I don't know…"

"About what? The talking, the touching, or both?"

"The touching part mostly, but I'm kind of nervous about the talking part too."

"Like I said, safewords apply. You've used them and they've worked so far, but it's up to you."

"I think I might be okay with the talking part."

"What are your safewords?"

"Yellow for I need something to change, or I need a minute, and red to bail."

"Good. It's no secret that you are submissive and I know there was a time when you physically participated in BDSM activities. If you felt safe, and had the opportunity, do you think you would like to dip your toe back in the BDSM pond?"

Mac took her time gathering her thoughts. This had to be one of the last questions she expected to be asked, but strangely, one that had been at the front of her mind for quite some time. "Yeah, I think so."

"Brave girl. The next question is a follow up on the last. What do you think would make you feel safe enough to try?"

In theory, this was easy. In practice, Mac wasn't so sure. "Sully would have to be there, no nudity, and no restraints."

Finn gave a slight chuckle. "You've given this a little thought."

"Yeah. Truth is, I still want it, but it scares me, so I've been living vicariously through Sully and the internet."

"Not very rewarding, is it?"

Mac shook her head. "No. Sully's been telling me for years that I've been letting the bastard win by letting his actions impose limits on my life. I know he's right, but it's only recently I've felt ready to try."

"Bonus question. Do you think you'd feel safe enough to try with me?"

"Maybe. When do I get to ask a question?"

"Okay, it's your turn to ask questions."

Mac's head was full of them, and almost every one pertained to her fear of not being enough, in some capacity or another. "Would you walk away from me if it turns out I can't play?"

"Remember earlier, we were talking about accepting people for who they are? Well, this is part of it. I want to exchange check-lists later, and when we do, I'm sure there will be things that are a hard limit for you that I enjoy. I'm also sure, there are going to be lots of things on that check-list that we both enjoy. I'm not willing to throw away an otherwise great relationship because of a few incompatibilities. I wouldn't worry about not being able to play. You may never be able to play in the way you used to, but there are plenty of ways to play."

"What if I can never have sex again?"

"Honey, let's not borrow trouble. Yes, you've got some issues that are complicating to a relationship. But I'm willing to put in whatever work is necessary to give you and me a real shot. It won't be easy, but I need to know you aren't going to run away when things get tough too."

"It's scary."

"I know, but sometimes the worthwhile things are. So, wanna go steady?"

Mac shot him a cheeky grin. "Do I get to wear your class ring?"

"Something like that."

There was something in the way he said it that made Mac suspect he was talking about a collar, so she decided to press. "Care to elaborate?"

"You'll get it when your ready for it."

Mac felt almost certain Finn meant a collar, and the idea excited her. "Okay, I'll go steady with you."

"You know that means kissing."

"I should hope so."

"I want to try something. This is a great position for snuggling, but for kissing? Not so much. Could you try lying on top of me?"

"Okay."

They shifted so Finn was lying on his back on the sofa with Mac on top, enfolded in Finn's arms. Before she'd even realised she was hyper-ventilating, Finn had shifted them to their sides with him positioned against the back of the sofa, leaving Mac an unobstructed escape route.

"Fuck, fuck, fuck." Mac buried her head beneath her arm as mortification branded her cheeks. She couldn't even lay on top of a guy without losing it. What kind of future could they possibly have?

"Hey, it's okay." Finn stroked up and down her arm. "You gave it a try. That's the worst part, you know. That first time you try something that scares you witless. You're dealing with some big shit. I know it's going to get in the way more often than not, and we'll deal with it all as it comes. Can you look at me?"

"No."

"Why not?"

"Because I'm too embarrassed."

"I don't know what you've got to be embarrassed about. I asked you to try something, and you did exactly what I asked. That's nothing to be embarrassed about. When a sub safewords after trying something, but it's too much, do you think that sub should feel embarrassed?"

"Of course not."

"Okay, let's look at what just happened as if it were a scene. We tried something you were unsure of, and as your Dom, I noticed you had a problem and called the scene before you had a chance to safeword. Do you think that you, as the sub, should feel embarrassed?"

Mac latched onto the words, your Dom, and felt a warm glow deep in her belly. Then she remembered he'd asked a question. "No."

"Remember when you asked me about what if you can't play, and I said there were all kinds of ways to play. While I didn't mean it to be, for all intents and purposes, that was a scene. And it was successful. Your Dom asked you to try something, and you did. Can you please look at me now?"

Mac rubbed her face on her sleeve, erasing the tears before she shifted and caught Finn's gaze.

He trailed a finger down her face. "Thank you for trying. That was a big, scary step and I'm proud of you."

Mac gave him an uncertain smile, unprepared for the comfort his words provided.

"So, is lying on top of me a soft or hard limit?"

She closed her eyes and let herself relive the feeling for a moment. Scary, but not crippling. "Soft limit."

"Good. When you fill in your check-list, you will add lying on top of me to your soft limits."

Mac nodded, and feeling bold, asked, "Can I sleep here tonight? Like we did last night?"

"Of course you can. We're going steady. But are you sure?"

"I want to try. I was fine last night and I want to see if I'll be fine again."

"Alright, but sweetie, you need to know that just being near you makes me hard, and while I try to keep my erection from touching you, I can't guarantee it while we're sleeping."

"I understand, and I did notice. Please don't any more. I'm not saying rub yourself on me every chance you get, for now anyway, but don't censor yourself. Not with actions, or words. I don't want you to tiptoe around my issues. I would rather deal with a bad reaction than miss out on any more life."

"You got it. Wanna go to bed now?" Finn waggled his eyebrows, making Mac giggle.

"Yeah, but I had better call Sully first and let him know. He'll worry, otherwise."

"You do that, and I'll go find you a t-shirt to sleep in and meet you upstairs.

FINN WAS ALREADY in bed reading by the time Mac arrived. He looked up from his book when she tapped on the door frame. "Silly girl, we're going steady. That means you don't have to knock. There's a t-shirt there on the end of the bed for you. Before you go change, What did Mr. Worry-wart have to say?"

"He called me a dirty stop-out."

"Mmm, lucky me. I'm rather partial to oboe playing dirty stop-outs. What else did he say?"

"Nothing of note beyond calling me names."

"You still okay?"

"A little nervous, but I think so."

"Good. Go get changed and come to bed. I grabbed your toothbrush from the guest bathroom and left it for you beside the sink"

"Thanks." Mac picked up the t-shirt and trundled off to the bathroom.

Finn gave up on his book. There was no way he could get his mind off the prospect of spending the night alone with her. It could end up anywhere between idyllic and disaster. He'd be thrilled if they ended up at any point on the idyllic side of that spectrum.

Finn beamed at Mac as she inched her way back into the bedroom. "Welcome back." He flipped the covers down in invitation. Mac perched on the edge of the bed for a moment before laying on her back, so tense, she seemed ready to levitate. "Sweetie, you need to let your muscles go a little, or you're going to be awfully sore tomorrow. Can I massage your shoulders a bit?"

"I don't know if this was such a good idea after all."

"Whatever you need, baby. You have safewords. Give me a colour."

"Yellow."

"Okay, yellow. What do you need?

"I don't know."

"Yes, you do. Take a breath and think about it for a minute. What is the problem, and what needs to happen?"

"I'm scared."

"Do you need a minute for the scared feeling to go away, or do we need to change something?"

"Dammit. I'm such a mess. I'm sorry, Finn. I should go home. I don't even know why I asked for this."

"Yeah, you are a mess, but we can work with mess. You asked for this because it's what you want. I agreed because it's what I want and what you need. If you really need to go home, then call red. We agreed on safewords, and you've been very good with yellow. Going home because this is too much is exactly when you should use red. Are you still yellow, or are you red?"

"I'm still yellow."

"Good. Back to what we need to do to get you back to green."

"I need a hug."

"That's an easy fix." Finn gently gathered Mac into his side and wrapped his arms around her. You are so brave, do you know that?"

"I don't feel brave. I feel like a flake."

"Being brave is doing something when it's scary. You've done so many things that scare you in the last week. I bet more than you've done in the last five years. Am I right?"

"Probably."

"Do you want to fall asleep like this, or should we try spooning?"

"That's a hard one."

Finn groaned. "You're killing me. If you were any other sub, you'd be getting punished for teasing me with sexual innuendo, but in your case, I think it's a positive step forward. For now."

Mac looked up at Finn's face and flashed him a cheeky grin. He smiled back and said, "Kiss me goodnight."

She stretched up and gave him a firm kiss on the mouth and held it for a second before burrowing herself into his side.

He caressed her cheek and said, "Thank you, love. I'll expect a good morning kiss upon waking. Sweet dreams, baby."

"Goodnight, Finn. Thank you for being patient with me."

"My pleasure. Now, sleep."

NINE

"Hɪ Mᴀᴄ, I just called to wish you luck for tonight."

"Thanks, Sully. How are you feeling?"

"Still fucking ouchy, but they keep insisting I will live. Some days, I'm not convinced."

"Don't over-do it. Our deal has an expiry date. I only agreed to the Christmas schedule, not one concert more, and you are already into me for two, count 'em, two very large favours to be named later."

"See, I knew you'd be reminding me at every opportunity. I'm almost sorry I called. So, enough with the small talk, how are things going with Finn? You've slept over every night this week."

Mac smiled. "Things are going fine. He's so tolerant and patient. If I were him, I'd have dumped my ass before I'd even picked it up."

"Stop getting down on yourself. I am so proud of you and how far you've come. You deserve good things, and I think Finn is one of them. Truth be told, I think he deserves you too. You're good people."

"While I have you on the phone, can I ask a favour?"

"Sure. Is this one of those to be named later favours I owe you?"

"Nope, because I think you're going to like this one."

"Lay it on me."

"A few nights ago, Finn asked me if I'd be willing to try a scene if I felt safe and had the opportunity. I told him I would, but no nudity, no restraints, and you had to be there. I want to try before the play party on Sunday. Will you help?"

"What does Finn say?"

"I haven't talked to him about it. I wanted to talk to you first because I want it to be a surprise, but I don't know if that's really feasible."

"You know I'll do whatever you need. I'll be honoured to help, but this isn't the kind of surprise you can spring on him. The three of us are going to have to have a long, detailed discussion about this. How about tomorrow over lunch. That should give you both time to be rested after tonight's concert, but provide plenty of time for us to figure it all out before you need to prepare for tomorrow night's gig."

"Thanks, Sully."

"You're welcome. Do you want to talk to Finn about this, or would you like me to do it."

"I'll do it."

"Good girl."

"I'll let that slide."

"Cheeky wench."

"Sully?"

"Yes, my sweet?"

"Thank you for always being there. I don't think I would have survived without you."

"You're welcome. Whatever you need, Mac. Always."

"Okay, enough. I'm getting all soppy. I've gotta go, it's almost show time."

"I'll see you at lunch tomorrow. I'll take a cab, so you don't need to worry about me when deciding where you'll be laying your head tonight."

"Alright. I'll see you tomorrow."

Mac turned around to see Finn and she gave him her biggest smile.

"What are you up to? That's not the usual smile you have for me."

"I wanted to wait until later, but I guess now is as good a time as any." Mac closed her eyes and let the words spill out as fast as she could. "I just got off the phone with Sully. I want a scene before Sunday's play party, and Sully has agreed to help. I wanted it to be a surprise, but Sully said it wasn't the kind of surprise one springs on you."

"Sully was right. I appreciate the sentiment, Mac, but, do you think you're ready for this?"

"I'm going to have to be ready some day, and Sunday is as good a day as any. Besides, it's not like you've haven't taken every opportunity to slip in a little D/s dynamic when you thought I wasn't looking."

"Guilty as charged. Okay, we can give it a go, but first we'll have to discuss our check-lists. We can go over them tonight when we get home. Also, we'll have to get together to talk it through with Sully."

"Already sorted. He's coming to lunch tomorrow. Oh shit. I really shouldn't have made plans for you and your house without checking. I'm sorry. Do you want me to call him back and reschedule?

"Stop and take a breath. It's fine. Yes, you should probably check with me before booking me or my house, but if I had something planned for tomorrow, you'd have known it, so no harm done."

TEN

Finn woke Mac by peppering her face with tiny kisses. Once her eyes were open, he settled in for a long, deep kiss. "Good morning, baby. You had a quiet night last night."

Mac's eyes lit up as she smiled. "I did. I'm a little surprised, considering I'm nervous about this afternoon."

"We'll take it all really slow. You'll know exactly how the scene is going to go. No surprises and no pressure. I've got your hard limits branded in my brain, but we'll go over them again with Sully before we start.

It occurred to me last night, we've never discussed your orgasms. You've slept here every night for a week. So, I know you haven't had any then, but have you been giving yourself orgasms when you are at your place?"

"I've been responsible for my own orgasm pretty much my whole life, so, yes, I've been taking care of business when I get home."

"That stops now. Regardless of whether or not we have sex, the only orgasms you get are the ones I let you have. Are we clear?"

Mac scowled."What's the big deal? God only knows when, or even if I'm ever going to have sex again, so..."

"Enough. Beyond the fact that I told you no, I do have a reason for denying you. How many orgasms do you give yourself a week, on average?"

"I dunno, between three and five a day, so twenty-one to thirty-five a week?"

"Do you ever go a day or more without?"

"Rarely. Orgasms make me happy, so I may as well be happy every day."

"I'm afraid you won't be getting that kind of happy for a while, sweetheart."

"You can't be with me all day every day, so what's to stop me from giving myself orgasms when you aren't around?"

"You know the answer to that, Mac. Do you trust me?"

"Yeah, actually I do."

"Do you trust me to make decisions that may not result in your immediate gratification?"

"I think so."

"Not good enough, Mac. If I'm your Dom, and let's face it, you said it yourself the other night, we've got some semblance of a D/s relationship, then your job as my sub is to obey me, or use your safeword."

"You have a fair point. And yes, I do trust you. I'm just not happy that you're taking my orgasms away."

"I'm not taking them away, I'm just deferring them. Don't worry, you'll get them back, and I think you will be much happier with them when you do."

"I'm going to trust you on this, but if what you claim doesn't come to pass, you may want to be very cautious in everything you do, and you may need to sleep with one eye open."

Finn chuckled. "I won't let you down, love. I promise."

"So, um, how long will I be orgasmless, anyway?"

"As long as I say you will. End of discussion."

"I could be certifiably insane by the end of the week, you know."

"I doubt it, but it's a chance I'm willing to take."

"I don't think I like you very much right now."

"Are you feeling deprived and needy already? When was your last orgasm?"

"Friday. I didn't have time yesterday. What little time I had at home was spent placating a very angry kitty."

"About Gounod. I think you should bring him to stay here. He's more than welcome. You sleep here every night, and while I could stay with you sometimes, except for poor Gounod being lonely, our current sleeping arrangements seem to be working. So, what do you say?"

"He might pee or poop somewhere inappropriate to make his displeasure known."

"That's okay, we'll steal a pair of Sully's shoes for him."

Mac struggled not to laugh, "Okay, we can try it for a week, but I reserve the right to safeword out and you'll have to be the one to steal Sully's shoes."

"Deal. I'm hungry. How about some breakfast?"

"A most excellent idea. Shall I make toast?"

"Absolutely. You're getting quite good at it."

"Make sure my bacon is extra crispy."

"As you wish. Now up with you, wench."

Mac absorbed the warmth of Finn's embrace as she tried to decide whether she was completely crazy, or just a little nuts. What was she thinking, asking for a scene? Red. One little word and it all goes away. Then what? The prospect of never knowing was becoming worse than taking a chance.

"You're thinking too hard, sweetie. Colour, please."

"I needed a minute with myself, but I'm green"

"Alright, love, just like we talked about. A nice simple over the knee spanking. You've got a bra and underwear on and Sully's here. I won't use restraints, but if you move your hands or legs, even an inch from where I put them, I will have to hold you down for your own safety. You can do this. Five smacks and we're done. Ready?"

"What if I said no?"

"Then we'd wait until you are ready or safeword out. Are you saying no?"

"I'm saying yes, I'm ready."

"Good girl.

"I'm going to go sit on that chair now. Sully is going to be sitting next to me so you can see his face. When I call you, come to me and lay over my lap. I'll use my hands to help you get into the right position, but as long as you stay still, I'll only rest my left hand on the small of your back. If you move, I'll need to use my leg to keep your legs still, and my hand will hold your hands at the small of your back. Understood?"

"Got it."

"Good girl."

Mac couldn't help feeling abandoned when Finn left for his chair. She was thankful he didn't make her wait too long before calling her because she was worried she'd wimp out.

Finn beckoned. "I'm ready for you, love." Mac took a couple of shaky breaths before walking across the room and laying herself over his lap. "Good girl. You're doing fine. I need you to shift forward so your hips are snug against my thigh and then extend your legs back with your knees straight. Bend your toes like you're wearing high heels and use them to support your legs."

"I don't know if I can do this. I feel like I'm going to topple over."

"You've got it exactly right. Don't worry love, you'll feel a lot more stable in just a minute. Now, I want you to stretch your hands to the floor until you can touch it with your palms... Perfect." Mac felt like she was playing some perverted version of Twister. Once Finn placed his hand on the small of her back, her universe righted itself. "Mac, safewords please?"

"Yellow for a minute or to change something, red to bail."

"Good, here we go." Mac waited for the first strike, but when it didn't come, she started to lift her head. "Don't move. I'll get to it on my time, not yours."

A pause, and then a hand rubbing circles over her ass-cheeks. The rubbing morphed into kneading, and back to rubbing. When the first blow finally came, it nearly took her breath away. She had been so wrapped up in the massage, she wasn't prepared for the smack itself, let alone the force of it.

"FUCK!"

"Give me a colour."

Mac paused for a minute and caught her breath. "Green. I'm green."

"Good girl. You'll learn to expect the unexpected."

The pain continued to bloom and her bottom warmed. Finn resumed her ass massage and just as she relaxed into it, he struck her other buttock.

"FUCK, that hurts." Mac sucked in a big breath and groaned.

"Colour, love."

"Green."

"Such a good girl. Only three more."

"Can we pretend we're done?"

"Not if you want to graduate from fantasy-land to the real world."

Mac was relieved when Finn went back to that nice rubbing massage, and almost reared up when he launched two more smacks in quick succession. One on each cheek. The only thing that stopped her was the tiny voice of self-preservation reminding her, moving meant restraint.

"FECKING GODDAM SON OF A FECKING BITCH!"

"Colour, Mac?"

"I'm fecking green, but that was mean."

"Think about where you are and what you've taken so far. Not just for me, but for yourself. Sweetheart, you are so amazing. You've had four really big swats and you didn't move. You came pretty close with those last two, but you didn't. We're down to the last one, okay? I won't make you wait this time."

Before she could answer, her ass was on fire. It was harder than the rest and right on her sit-spot.

"I don't like you very much right now."

"That's okay. You will again later, and I can wait. Up you get." Finn wrapped a blanket around her and led her to the after-care area. He sat down and pulled her into his lap, mindful of her tender bottom. Mac snuggled in and automatically opened her lips to the water-bottle Finn held there. She drank greedily, not realising how thirsty she was. When she'd had enough, she pulled her head away, and accepted the small piece of chocolate Finn slipped into her mouth. She sucked on it as she let her mind hover into nothingness.

Finn caught Sully's eye and motioned his head as an invitation to join them on the sofa. "What do you think, Sully?"

"Almost perfect. So much better than I dared hope for. She was focused entirely on you. While I'd like to think that was because she trusts you completely, I suspect it was more because subconsciously, she knew I was here and it was safe to let go."

"Yeah, that's pretty much what I thought too, and I'm good with that. Whatever it takes, right?"

Sully tapped his finger on his chin. "Yeah. You'll do."

"Cheeky fuck."

"I'm going to go rest on the fainting couch for a while. I want to be wide awake for the evening's entertainment. If I can't play, I intend to collect plenty of wank-fodder."

Finn hugged Mac a little tighter and buried his nose in her hair as he murmured, "How are you doing, baby? Are you awake yet?"

"I did good?"

"You were perfect, sweetheart. How do you feel?"

"Relaxed."

Finn chuckled. "Yes, you are." He gently tapped her temple with his index finger. "But what about in here?"

"Quiet."

"Excellent."

"I don't think I want to play at the party."

"It's all up to you. Do you want to sit and watch like last time, or do you need to be completely away from it?"

"I want to watch. I'm not up for others seeing me vulnerable."

"Whatever you need. Now rest for a bit."

With such a successful afternoon in the playroom, that night Finn decided to push a little harder. "Mac, it's time for you to get used to us being naked and touching. I know you don't feel safe playing naked, so we won't. But from now on, unless you safeword, we sleep naked and shower together. That means washing each other."

"You don't mean right now, do you?"

"Yes, I mean right now."

"Can't we wait until tomorrow so I can have some time to get used to the idea?"

"No. You're more likely to work yourself up and talk yourself out of it. You'll undress me, but I'll let you remove your own clothes." Finn placed his hand at the small of Mac's back and urged her towards the bathroom. "Come on, love, time to go." Mac shuffled in front of him, but stopped in the bathroom doorway. "Colour, Mac?"

"Yellow."

"Okay. What do you need?"

Mac clenched and unclenched her fists a few times before responding. "I need a minute."

"Okay, take all the time you need." Finn traced lazy circles up and down her back until she resumed her trek to the shower. "So brave, sweetheart. Here's your only choice. Do you want to undress me first, or yourself. You don't need to speak. Your choice will be reflected in your actions."

Finn watched as Mac's face contorted with indecision. Relief washed over him when she didn't safeword, but instead reached forward, grasped the bottom of his t-shirt and lifted it. He beamed at her as he bent down so she could get it over his head and free of his arms. "You're doing great, love."

Mac dropped the shirt on the floor, and after a few false starts, she managed to fumble the button of Finn's jeans open. Her fingers trembled as she slid the zipper down, and she took a sharp intake of breath when she discovered he wasn't wearing underwear. She finally slipped his jeans to his ankles and off each foot. He stood naked before her, humbled by her triumphant grin. "Nicely done, sweetness. I'll get the shower warmed up and you can join me once you're undressed."

Finn monitored Mac's progress through the frosted glass of the shower stall, ready to deal with any sign of hesitance or indecision. He was pleased that, while slow, her progress was steady. He opened the door for her just as she reached it. "In you come, baby. The water is nice and warm." Finn shifted and Mac stepped into the spray.

"Let's get your hair wet so I can wash it first. Then I'll wash your body while we let the conditioner work its magic." Finn massaged Mac's scalp as he shampooed her hair. Her moans of pleasure were almost enough to send him over the edge.

"Let's rinse, then we'll condition." Mac tipped her head back, eyes closed and held still until the water ran clear down her back.

Finn caressed her cheek. "Time for conditioner, love." He worked the conditioner into her hair with the same care as he had the shampoo. When he was sure her hair was completely slathered, he guided her out of the spray. "Stand there. I want your feet shoulder width apart and then I want you to stay perfectly still. I'll move you as needed.

Mac nodded and Finn grabbed a wash-cloth and loaded it with shower gel. He started at her neck and lathered his way across her left shoulder, down her arm to her fingertips. He returned to her neck and did the same for her right side. "I'm going to do your back now, okay?"

"Okay."

"Good girl." Finn moved behind her and rubbed the cloth side to side from her neck to the top of her buttocks. "It's time to do your bum now, love. Deep breath, and let it out slowly."

Mac did as she was told. She flinched a little as Finn rubbed her tender cheeks, but held her ground. Finn wasn't surprised when she tensed as he began to ease her buttocks apart. "Another deep breath, Mac. You're doing great. Washing your body is all that's going to happen to you. I promise." Mac took another deep breath, and her muscles relaxed a little as she let it out. "Good girl. I'm going to do your front now."

Finn moved to face her and started at her neck again, this time, working down her chest. She seemed relatively calm, so he lingered over her breasts for a moment, purposely avoiding her nipples. He felt a jolt of satisfaction as her nipples puckered and she let out a frustrated groan. He continued his journey south, stopping just shy of her pubis.

"Okay, gorgeous, we're in the home stretch. I'm going to do your legs now, but I'm going to start at your toes and work my way up. You can place a hand on the wall if you feel unsteady."

Finn crouched at Mac's feet. He lifted her left and washed it thoroughly before moving up her leg until he was nearly at the top. He did the same to the other and then rose to face her. "Remember, sweetheart, I'm just washing you. Nothing more. Okay?"

"Yeah."

Finn kept his eyes on Mac's as he slipped his hands between her legs. Her mouth opened slightly and she closed her eyes as he gently spread her pussy lips between his thumb and forefinger, letting them brush against her clit. He held them open while he used the cloth in his other hand to wash her. When she tried to tilt her pelvis towards the cloth, he pulled it away. "There, all done. Time to get you all rinsed off now, love."

Finn guided her back under the spray. "Well done, Mac. You may do whatever you need to get rid of all the soap, but don't spend too long on your pussy. You don't have my permission to do anything more than rinse it. Clear?"

"Clear."

"Good. Once you're done, it's your turn to wash my body. You may do it any way you want, but you must wash my entire body."

Mac's lip quivered. "Everything?"

"Everything. You'll be fine. You have safewords. Use them if you need them." He was glad that Mac didn't dawdle over rinsing. He was anxious to get her to bed and move on to the next part of his plan.

While she clearly struggled with a lot of the things they did together, her determination to conquer her fears was inspiring. It was this tenacity that convinced him she could, and would, heal enough for them to enjoy a normal, healthy sex life together. He wasn't a fool, he knew it was going to take a lot more time and patience, but the deeper she burrowed into his heart, the more confident he felt she was worth it.

Mac's hands on his chest brought Finn back from his thoughts. "Done?"

"Yeah. I'm ready to wash you now."

"First, this." Finn took Mac's face in his hands and kissed her gently. "I am proud of you, sweetness. We're almost done."

"Finn, can you close your eyes while I do this? I've never done this, not even before...I think I might find it easier if you aren't watching me."

"Whatever you need, as long as you do it, or safeword."

"Thanks. Can you bend down a bit so I can reach your head?"

Finn settled himself on the floor of the shower, eyes closed, kneeling up in front of Mac so she could easily reach his head to wash his hair. She was quick, but thorough, and his scalp felt tingly when she was done. She took the same cloth Finn used, and added more shower gel. She washed as much of his upper-body as she could comfortably reach before asking him to rise.

Mac's hands over his body sent Finn's cock into overdrive. She came to an abrupt halt just above his navel, and concerned, he opened his eyes and looked down at her. "Honey, it's just a body part. No different than my foot, or my toe, or my hand, or my nose."

"It can hurt me."

"It can, but if you don't want it to, I won't let it. I promise. My hand hurt you today, but only because you said it could. Same thing with my penis. In case you haven't noticed, it's been like this pretty much since I opened the door the night we met. And while it's generally in charge of whether it's up or down, I'm in charge of everything else. Do you trust me to do everything I can to keep you safe?"

"Yeah. It's just sometimes I get freaked out."

"I know, and that's okay. We're going to have a lot of ups and downs, both good and bad. As long as somewhere deep inside, you trust that I'll do everything in my power to keep you as safe as Sully does, then everything is going to be fine. I promise."

"You make a lot of promises."

"Only those I can keep. Are you ready to continue?"

"Yes. Close your eyes again, please."

Finn closed his eyes and it took everything he had to

keep from coming when she lathered his balls and stroked the sudsy cloth up and down his shaft. Finn reached down and touched her hand. "Mac, fair warning, if you keep that up, I'm going to come, and I don't think you're ready for that. I'm clean enough.

"What if I want to make you come?"

"That's very generous of you, but I think we'll leave that for another time. Now, let's get finished. I'm tired and would like to get to bed soon."

Mac finished up fairly quickly. Finn wasn't surprised that once she'd got past the part of his body she was most scared of, the rest was easy. "Well done, love. You can enjoy the shower while I dry off. Then, when you come out, I'll towel you off and blow your hair dry."

ELEVEN

A whole feckin' week without an orgasm. Mac was feeling needy, and Finn, the bastard, seemed to always know when she was on the verge of taking the edge off. Every time she thought she'd sneak away, he diverted her attention to something else. She was sure she really would go crazy if she didn't get some relief soon. She finally stopped complaining about it when he warned her he'd make her wait an extra day for every time she brought the subject up. That wasn't a chance she was willing to take.

To make matters worse, he touched her everywhere except where she really wanted. He would always get so close she thought it would happen, then poof, gone. It was like he had sexual attention deficit disorder.

She'd hoped giving him an orgasm in the shower every night might encourage him to reciprocate, but every time she tried, he stopped her. Then he'd wait until she was finished washing him, before giving himself an orgasm and making her rewash his lower body. Fucker.

Mac was greeted by a far too cheerful Finn as she entered the kitchen.

"Good morning. How come you're scowling, love?"

Mac pasted an insincere smile to her face. "I'm not scowling. I'm a happy, happy girl." His chuckle brought her scowl back before she could to stop it.

Finn held out a mug. "Come and get some tea, grumpy-girl." Mac grudgingly accepted the tea and sat at the table.

Finn sat in the chair beside her and took a long sip of his coffee. "Mac, it's time to talk about some things. I need to know if you can put the grumpy on hold for a few minutes or so." Mac shrugged, then nodded. "That wasn't very convincing, love. Wanna try again?"

"Yes. What do you want to talk about?"

"Let's start with Christmas. Sully says you spend it alone every year."

"Not quite, I have Gounod. That's how I like it, and that's how it's going to stay."

"I host an afternoon gathering and pot-luck supper for friends who would otherwise spend it alone. I cook a turkey and everyone else brings the fixings. You're on dessert. Please, for the love of everything that's holy, don't make it yourself. Store-bought will be fine.

"Maybe you didn't hear me. I spend my Christmas with Gounod, so you'll have to assign store-bought dessert to someone else."

"I did hear you, sweetness. Christmas is three days away, we have a concert tomorrow night, and Gounod is here. You're both settled. Is spending a lonely Christmas in your house with only Gounod for company worth uprooting the two of you for a single night?"

"Who says it would be only one night? My obligation to Dominant Cord is over when the last note has been played tomorrow night."

"Sweetheart, you sleep here because we're going

steady, which is not limited to your time with Dominant Cord. We like each other, we trust each other, and we agreed to do whatever is necessary to give whatever this is we have, a real shot. I know it's scary. But it's just the next scary thing in the long line of scary things you've faced in recent weeks."

"I don't know."

"That's an improvement on no. How about we call this yellow for now. You can take some time with it, and if it's still yellow in the morning, then we'll see if we can come up with changes we can both live with. Okay?"

Mac felt miserable. She was mixed up. She'd spent so many Christmases alone, it was what she was comfortable with, but she couldn't lie to herself. Every one of those lonely Christmases had her wishing she had someone special she could spend it with. Sully was wonderful, but she relied on him too much as it was, she couldn't allow her hangups and problems to taint Christmas with his family. "Okay, let's hold off until the morning."

"Good. Next order of business. Play party tonight."

"I won't be playing."

"Okay. Can we have a small scene this afternoon?"

"What kind of scene?"

"A slight variation on the one from last week. Either you take your spanking naked with Sully here, or you keep your bra and panties, but no Sully." It took Mac a few seconds to absorb what Finn was asking. Naked around Sully, or scene without him? What an impossible choice. "You have safewords, baby. They work anytime, including right now, but I'm going to change this one up a little. Yellow is only for more time, but you will have to choose one of the two options I gave you. Otherwise, you have to call red."

"Yellow."

"Good girl. Give Sully a call and talk it through with him. I'm sure that'll help with your decision. I'm going to go get things organised in the playroom."

———

Mac absently stroked Gounod. "And now, I don't know what to do."

"Sweetie, what does your heart say?" Sully asked.

"lub-dub, you prick."

"Such a funny girl."

"My heart tells me I need to wean myself off of you."

"I knew you'd get there one day."

Macs chest tightened. "I'm sorry I've been such a burden."

"Stop it. You've never, ever been a burden. All I did was hold the back of the bike until you felt safe enough for me to let go. That's what love is, sweetheart. You'd do exactly the same for me."

"No question."

"So, will you tell me how the rest of my day is going, so I can plan accordingly."

Mac knew it was time to let Sully release the back of her bike. "You're off the hook. I'll see you tonight. I love you."

"I love you too."

———

At the sound of Mac on the stairs, Finn put down the chair he was carrying and sat in it while he waited for her to appear.

"There you are love. Did you talk to Sully?"

"Yeah. Thanks for the suggestion, it helped."

"And? Have you picked an option?"

"No Sully."

Finn decided not to give her a chance to over-think it. "In that case, there's no time like the present. Strip to your bra and panties or safeword."

Mac started with her shirt and made slow steady progress as Finn looked on in anticipation. As the last piece of clothing fell to the floor, he said, "You can leave them there, but in future, you will fold your clothes and set them down neatly when I tell you to strip."

"Sorry."

"No need to apologise. It's not something we've discussed, so it's not something I would reasonably expect. Come here and position yourself exactly the way you were last time."

Mac crossed the floor and laid herself over Finn's lap without hesitation. Finn felt she wiggled a little too much as she settled into position. She was becoming quite a tease, but he didn't feel the need to correct her like he would any other sub. He found he really didn't care whether it was her past, or her personality that allowed him to tolerate behaviour bordering on bratty. There would still be consequences, but they would be the sort to limit the behaviour, not obliterate it.

"Are you quite settled, Mac?" She wiggled again, and Finn knew it was deliberate. He almost felt guilty at the pleasure he'd get from giving Mac her first real punishment. Putting his sadistic tendencies aside hadn't been much of a hardship, but the chance to explore Mac's pain threshold as a result of her own behaviour was too good to pass up. "Mac, I think you're wiggling around more you need to. Am I right?"

"Maaaaybe."

"I need a straight answer, love."

"Yes, but it was too tempting."

"There are many things about you I find too tempting, but I control myself. I think you purposely wiggled more than necessary when you first got yourself settled. I'll give you that one for free, but what came after, you'll have to pay for at the end of the scene. I'm feeling generous, so I will give you two options. You may either have two extra smacks with my hand on your bare bum, or five strokes with a tawse over your panties. Pick one."

"Bare bum."

Finn was relieved. While his intention was to give Mac options designed to help her work through issues stemming from the attack, he knew there was every possibility it could backfire. He never offered her a choice he wasn't prepared to follow through on, but so far, he'd been lucky. "Just like last time, I won't hold you down as long as you stay still. Clear?"

"Clear."

"Safewords?"

"Yellow to pause, red to bail."

"Here we go, then."

Finn rubbed, squeezed and kneaded Mac's ass, and the moment her glutes went slack, he brought his hand down once on each cheek and resumed his massage.

"OWWWWW! YOU HURT ME!"

"Breathe through it, love. You've got a ways to go yet and I'm just getting warmed up."

"I don't like you any more. That nice massaginess doesn't feel so nice any more. You're mean."

"I know." Finn continued massaging. He waited until her ass-cheeks relaxed, before giving her another two hard smacks and more massage.

"FUCK!"

"Breathe, baby. Just breathe. One more of these, then

we'll get your punishment out of the way. After that, we can go have a snuggle, and you can have some chocolate from your favourite shop."

"I don't care. I hate you and I hate chocolate."

"I know, sweetheart."

"Don't feckin' patronise me"

"Enough, Mac. I'll tolerate some rudeness because you are taking pain for me, and if that's what it takes to get you through it, then I'll go with it for now. But you took it too far. Now you know where the line is, cross it, and there will be consequences. Clear?"

"Clear."

Finn rubbed Mac's ass gently, but he only gave her a few seconds before he nailed her in her sit-spot.

"THAT FECKING HURTS!"

"I know, honey, but now you've got two more and these ones are punishment."

"I'm really sorry I wiggled to tease you."

"I believe you. That doesn't get you out of it, though. I'll always give you any punishment you earn. There might be times when I will defer it, but I promise I'll always give it to you."

"That's one promise I would be perfectly happy if you didn't keep."

"Enough stalling. Let's get this over with, I want to snuggle with you."

"Fine."

"Good girl. Now stay still, I'm going to slip your panties down just enough so they don't block where I'll be spanking. Colour?"

"I'm green."

"Good girl." Finn shifted and caught hold of the sides of Mac's panties. He wiggled and pulled until they were completely clear of her ass. The crotch was soaked. This counted for multiple points in favour of going ahead with his after party plans.

Normally, he would let some tension mount, but Mac was at green and with this being her first punishment, he wanted to keep things as positive as he could. He hauled his arm back and smacked her full-force on the sit-spot of her left side, and before she had a chance to register the pain, he did the same to her right, then pulled up her panties. Her deep intake of breath told him, it was going to be one long, loud scream.

He waited patiently until her lungs were empty before speaking. "All done, baby, but you need to breathe through the pain. Now up we get. I've got a nice cosy blanket just for you. We'll go have a snuggle on the sofa and you can have some water and chocolate."

Finn wrapped Mac in her blanket, and carried her across to the sofa, careful of her sore ass as he settled her on his lap. He reached for a bottle of water and lifted it to her lips. It was then, he finally got a good look at her face. Tears streamed, but her eyes twinkled and relief washed over him. He hadn't totally fucked up.

He let Mac suck back water until she pulled away from the bottle on her own. He smirked a little when she looked at him, her eyes expectant and her mouth open. "Oh honey, right now, looking at your mouth open like that makes me want to feed my cock to you one inch at a time."

"Chocolate. You promised chocolate, and you said you always keep your promises."

"Cock? Yes, I would happily give you cock."

"Finn, please don't tease me. You promised me good chocolate."

"Yes, I did, and you told me you hate chocolate. I should deprive you and feed you cock instead for uttering such a blatant untruth, but I'll accept that it falls within acceptable boundaries when you're taking pain for me." Finn slid a square of chocolate into his mouth, and slipped it into Mac's with his tongue as he kissed her.

"Mmmm, best chocolate delivery method ever."

"I'm looking forward to showing you all of my chocolate delivery methods. When your ready for more, just wiggle your bum."

MAC WAS STARTLED out of her reverie by Sully's voice. "You're looking a little dreamy, Mac"

"Hey, you're kind of early, aren't you?"

"Yeah, I may have let go of the back of your bike, but that doesn't mean I didn't need to check up on you in case you fell off."

"Thanks. You are a sweet man. If only we could find you a nice subby-type who likes having her feet played with."

"Let's keep that on hold until my ribs are better."

"I'm just poking. I would beat you myself if you tried to play while you're messed up."

"Enough about me and not playing. I want to know all about how it went with you today?"

"Actually, it was good. I didn't freak out and I didn't safeword. Not even yellow. Not only that, I earned a punishment and I took it."

"Oh Mac, I'm so proud of you. Hang on, punishment? What punishment?"

"I teased Finn by being wigglier than I should when I was settling in for our scene and he called me on it. I had the choice between two with his hand on my bare ass, or five with a tawse over my panties. I went with the bare ass."

Sully chuckled. "Very, very wise choice, sweetheart. Your panties wouldn't have provided any protection from a tawse, and trust me, whatever you got from Finn's hand wasn't anything close to the pain you'd have felt from the tawse. And, you'd have felt that pain five times, not two."

"I kind of figured."

"Are you really okay, though?"

"Yeah, I am. I know you're going to shower me with smuggery and 'I told you so,' but you were right. The more scary things I do, the less scary the next one seems."

"Sweetie, my pride in you is boundless. You are amazing, and you deserve to break free of the box you built around yourself. Now, enough sap. It's supper-time, and I brought your favourite."

TWELVE

FINN NEVER GOT TIRED of seeing Mac in his bed, waiting for him to join her. He smiled and slipped in beside her. "How would you like an orgasm tonight?"

"I would kill for an orgasm tonight."

"No need to go that far, although, you may come to regret your decision."

"No, I really want an orgasm, and I'll do pretty much anything to get one."

"I noticed when I pulled your panties down for your last two spanks this afternoon, they were very, very wet. What do you think caused that?"

"I don't know."

"Don't know, or don't want to say?"

"Don't want to say."

"Fair enough. How about I make a little guess and you nod if I get it right?"

"I can do that."

"I think your panties were soaking wet because that spanking made you horny. Is that true?" Mac nodded and Finn continued. "What I didn't get an opportunity to assess, was whether those last two smacks killed your horniness, increased your horniness, or had no effect. So, just nod when I get to the right answer. More horny?" Mac gave another nod. "This makes things interesting. Here's the plan. I will let you have an orgasm and you will even get to choose the method — the catch is, you may only choose from the options I give you. Still want an orgasm?"

"Like you wouldn't believe."

"Safewords?"

"yellow to pause, red to bail."

"Good. Here are your options, you may have one orgasm from my mouth while I inflict all manner of pain, or you may have three orgasms from a vibrator while I have my cock buried deep inside you."

Mac groaned. "You're enjoying this way too much."

Finn grinned. "Of course. I'm a sadist. I'm waiting."

"Jeez. I don't know. One orgasm if I take pain, or three orgasms if I let you fuck me."

"I never said anything about fucking you. I said you'd have them with my cock inside you."

"You would just leave it there without moving?"

"That's exactly what I'd do. I'm betting your vibrator sees more action than I'm proposing for my cock."

"That doesn't make it any less terrifying."

"I know, love. Either way, you'll get at least one orgasm, but you have to work for it."

"What if I can't do it?"

"You have safewords."

"But if I call red, I won't get my orgasm."

"Correct. However, you can call yellow and try your other option first."

"So, if I try one option, but end up not being able to deal, I still have a chance to get my orgasm if I call yellow and switch options?"

"That's precisely what I'm saying. If, however, you can't deal with the other option either, you will have to wait until I offer you another opportunity to earn an orgasm."

"You are diabolical."

"And your point is?"

There was a long silence before Mac finally spoke, her voice, shaky. "I'm sorry, Finn. I can't do it. Red."

Finn wasn't surprised, more relieved. He'd been pushing her so hard, he had concerns over whether he could trust her to know when to call red. He smiled and stroked her hair."Good for you."

Mac's eyes went wide in confusion. "You aren't mad?"

He kissed the tip of her nose. "Of course not. You have the power, love. It's yours to give, and yours to take back. Right now it's all yours. It's been a pretty heavy day for you, sweetheart. Are you ready to get some sleep?"

"You are mad."

"No, I'm not mad at all. I'm adjusting tonight's plans, nothing more. Is there something else you want to do before we go to sleep?"

"Can we cuddle?"

Finn pulled Mac into his side and held her close as he gently stroked her face. "Always."

IT WAS STILL DARK when Finn woke to a hand snaking its way down his torso. He grabbed it before it reached his navel. He reached over and switched on the light. "It's the middle of the night. What's going on, love?"

"I was thinking about earlier, when I called red."

"Okay, what about it?"

"I let that bastard win tonight. He made me scared of sex, and that fear deprived me of an orgasm or three. I don't want him to have that kind of power over me any more."

"What do you want to do about it?"

"Aw, fuck. I want three orgasms, no pain, and I want to be able to have a normal sex life."

Finn was conflicted. He so desperately wanted to agree, but he didn't want this to end up making things worse for her. Caution won out. "I don't know about this, love. I think we should hold off for a bit to give you more time to get used to the idea."

"No. I've been thinking about it for hours. You said all you'll ever ask me to do is try, and I want to try."

"Okay. If you're sure, we can try, but you have to promise to call red if you are even a little bit uncomfortable."

"I promise."

"Good. Just like a scene, I'm going to give you the details up front. No surprises, I promise."

"Okay."

"I am going to lay here on my back with my hands at my side, and you are going to sit on my cock. You may go as slowly as you need, but you may only travel downward unless you safeword. Once I am completely inside you, I'm going to need to use my hands for the vibrator, okay?"

"As okay as it's going to get."

"Fair enough. One more choice before we begin. Do you want to put the condom on, or shall I?"

"I want to do it."

Finn turned and opened the drawer of his bedside table. From it, he extracted a condom, a Rabbit and a bullet. He turned back to Mac and handed her the condom. He grinned as he held up the Rabbit. "A birdie told me this is your vibrator of choice, but I think the bullet will better serve our purpose tonight. "

"I don't know whether to thank that birdie, or give all his shoes to Gounod."

Finn chuckled. "Okay, love, one last thing before you put my condom on. Are you wet, or do we need lube?"

"Believe it or not, I'm totally wet."

"Show me." Mac flushed, but dipped a finger inside and held it in front of him. He opened his mouth and she slipped her wet finger in. Finn moaned as he sucked her finger clean before releasing it. She was killing him. "Honey, I sure like the taste of things to come. Condom, please."

Mac opened the packet and removed the condom before kneeling beside Finn. She rolled it onto his cock and winked, looking pleased with herself when she was done. "There."

"Good girl. Whenever you're ready." She shifted so she had one knee either side of Finn's body. It took all his concentration to stay perfectly still while he watched Mac struggle with her task "Colour, Mac?"

"Greenish Yellow?"

"Okay. Not a standard response, but we'll go with it. We're on your time, baby. No hurry."

"Oh, we're in a hurry, pal. I want my feckin' orgasms, dammit."

"Alrighty, then." Finn watched Mac briefly close her eyes before reaching down and grasping the base of his cock. She held it steady as she positioned herself so the tip was touching her entrance. "Colour?"

"I'm surprisingly green."

Finn watched Mac's pussy swallow his cock one agonising inch at a time. He fought his need for control, his arms rigidly at his sides, bullet clenched in his fist. The minute she bottomed out, he had the vibrator on and positioned over her clit.

"I'm going to come, I'm going to come..." The bullet buzzed against her clit and Mac let out a low moan as her world exploded in a kaleidoscope of colour.

"Two more, baby."

Mac leaned forward, placing her hands on Finn's chest for support as she undulated her hips to increase the pressure of the vibrator on her clit. The pleasure built again and she whined as her pelvis jerked uncontrollably.

"There you go, sweetheart. Last one."

Mac wasn't sure she had another in her. She didn't think she'd come so hard in her life. Maybe there was something to this whole orgasm deferral thing.

Finn's eyes twinkled. "Honey, if you can think, I'm not doing my job properly."

The speed of the vibrator increased and she was completely overwhelmed by the sensation. "Stop, stop, stop, please stop. I can't take any more."

FINN IMMEDIATELY KILLED the vibrator and replaced his hands at his sides. His first instinct was to pull Mac off him, but he was terrified that touching her would be worse than leaving her be, so he remained perfectly still. "Colour, love?"

"Yellow."

"Good. What do you need?"

"I need a hug"

"Okay. Do you want to climb off me first?"

"No. I'm okay. Actually, I like how you feel inside me. I just couldn't take another orgasm."

"In that case, how about you lay yourself down on my

chest and I'll give you that hug. You can have the last orgasm another time."

Mac lay down with her right cheek resting on Finn's chest. He wrapped his arms around her back and tilted his head forward to kiss the top of her head.

"What about you?" Mac asked.

"What about me?"

"You must be going nuts, being inside me and not coming."

"I'm fine. I am so proud of you right now, I could burst."

"I'm proud of me too."

"Good girl. Are you ready for sleep now?"

"Almost. I want you to come inside me first."

"That's thoughtful of you, sweetness, but—"

"Please, Finn. I want to try more. I'm feeling really brave right now, even without feeling insanely needy. Like you keep saying, I've got safewords."

Finn let Mac go and set his hands back at his sides. "You're in charge."

"In that case, please put your hands on my hips and take control."

"Honey, I don't want to take any chances with you."

"I'm asking you to. I'm being clear in what I want. Please?"

Finn knew he wouldn't last long, and he was grateful. Maybe this wasn't a bad idea. After all, he and Sully had been after her to push her boundaries. "Alright. You have your safewords, but I want you to keep your hands on mine and pull on them if you need me to let go of you."

"Okay."

Finn started with his hands on Mac's knees and slid them up her legs until they rested on her hips. Mac put her hands over them and squeezed. "You can hold them harder than that."

"You told me I was in control. This is how it's going to be. This time. Eyes on me." Finn fixed his eyes on Mac's as he held her hips still and gently pumped himself in and out of her body. With a wicked smile, she began clenching her inner muscles and it was all over. His hands tightened on her hips and he thrust wildly, finally holding her hard to him as his orgasm subsided.

As sanity returned, Finn realised what he'd done and tried to pull his hands from Mac's hips. "Baby, I'm so sorry."

Mac grinned and held his hands in place for a moment before letting go and laying back down on his chest. "There's nothing to be sorry for. It was wonderful and amazing."

"Honey, you didn't come."

"No, not this time. But after those first two orgasms, I don't feel deprived. I think it might even be better that I didn't. The last time a man was inside me I didn't come either. For obvious reasons. Apparently, not only can I have sex, it doesn't have to be wrapped in an orgasm for me to enjoy it."

"Did you really enjoy it?"

"Yeah. I did. I think I might want to do that again, really soon."

"I may need a little recovery time. You blew more than my mind, love."

"Good."

Finn knew sex wasn't always going to go so smoothly, but this first time being such a success had him cautiously optimistic about their future. There was still a plethora of sexual land mines to navigate, and for the short-term, they would have a detailed plan for each sexual encounter, even though it would not be part of a scene. That fucker did a good job of tainting sex and bondage for Mac. Perhaps one day, they'd get her to a point where she could handle being restrained and maybe even during sex, he mused. Slow down and deal with sex first.

Mac's voice brought him out of his head. "You're thinking awfully hard. What's the matter?"

"Just thinking about the future."

"Anything you'd care to share with me?"

"Sure. I was thinking about sex."

"Mmmm. What about it?"

"That we're going to have lots more of it, but we need to be prepared for issues to come up, and accept them as part of the process. We'll have to explore and experiment in order to establish your limits. While what we just shared was incredible, neither of us will be satisfied with what we did tonight being the only dish on the menu."

"I know, and I trust you."

"That means everything to me, baby. I need to get rid of this condom before we have a problem. Can you please lift off slowly?" Finn slipped his hand between their bodies and held the condom in place as Mac raised herself up and over to Finn's side. "I'll be back in just a minute, sweetheart. You stay put. I'll bring a nice warm cloth to clean you up.

Mac had barely started her second cup of tea before Finn resurrected their discussion of Christmas plans.

"We agreed that you'd give me an answer this morning."

"You don't let anything go, do you?"

"Nope. A deferral is the best you can hope for. So?"

After so much upheaval in her life lately, Mac was tempted to escape it by continuing her solo Christmas routine. However, deep down she knew it would be a disaster. She felt safe and alive when she was with Finn. Being home alone, at best made her feel numb. "I guess I'll be hunting and gathering dessert."

"Excellent. Last concert tonight. I'll miss having you play with Dominant Cord, but lucky for me, I can play with you any time I like, day or night. Finn waggled his eyebrows and stole a kiss.

THIRTEEN

MAC SLIPPED out of Finn's bed. She had to get away and think. She grabbed her robe and slipped it on as she tiptoed from the room. Tea. She'd ruminate over a quiet cup of tea.

Gounod wove between her feet as she put the kettle on. She absently bent and picked him up, as she scratched beneath his chin. "What do you think, little brat?"

"I don't know what he thinks, but I'm thinking, why aren't you in bed where you belong?"

Mac nearly dropped the cat as she spun to face Finn. "I couldn't sleep."

"Apparently. What's wrong, love?"

"Probably final concert adrenalin pumping through my veins."

"Sit down." Mac did as she was told and Finn took a seat next to her. "Let's try again. What's wrong?"

"I don't know. I feel all mixed up. One minute I'm happy and life's great, the next, I feel like I'm making a huge mistake and my world is going to explode. We're done with the Christmas concerts and I don't know why I'm still here."

"Sweetheart, you're here because that's what we both want. This is between you and me on a personal level. The only way this connects professionally is how we met. I know you're scared. You've got all kinds of good reasons to be, but we're working on them. Together."

"I don't know. I keep feeling like I should go home."

Finn laid a hand over Mac's. "What do you have waiting for you there?"

"My life."

"Tell me what that life has that you can't have here?"

"Control. I have no control here."

"You have all the control, love. Nothing happens you don't want. You may give me your power, but you can take it away with a single word. You've proven that."

"No, I mean, at home, my life was ordered exactly how I like it."

"Really? You still haven't answered me. What does that life have that you can't have here?"

"Fuck, I don't know. I just want to run away to where I feel safe."

"What makes that life more safe than this one?"

Mac was irritated. He was worse than a bloody shrink with all this probing. "I don't know. Stop asking me these questions. I just want to run away."

"Honey, you've been on your own for a really long time. You've only ever had Sully to rely on, and I suspect you didn't lean on him nearly enough. Being alone is what you're used to, so that's what makes you feel comfortable and safe. I get that.

"This is pretty scary for me too. It's been a long time since I've committed to more than a scene or two and some sex. You're the first person I've been serious about since I lost my wife. When we first got together, you were worried about me running from you. Look at me. I'm right here, Mac, and I'm not leaving. Give us a chance and stay. Please?"

Mac looked at Finn, a tear trickling down her cheek. "You're right, I'm terrified. What if this doesn't work out? What if you come to hate me?"

Finn wiped the tear away. "Then we deal. No more borrowing trouble."

"I don't know if I can do this, Finn."

"I'm not asking you to do this. I'm only asking you to try."

Mac nodded and Finn pulled her into his lap, wrapping his arms around her. "Let me take you back to bed. We're both exhausted. Things will look better in the morning."

FOURTEEN

FINN TRAILED a finger down Mac's back. "Santa comes tonight."

"I just bet he does."

After her emotional upheaval the previous night, Finn was glad to see she'd regained some spunk. "Careful, or he might not let you come with him."

"Sorry Santa."

"You just might be." Finn cupped Mac's face in his hand. "Remember when I asked you to go steady and you asked if you get to wear my class ring?"

"Yeah, you said, 'Something like that,' as I recall."

He released her face and took her hand. In it, he placed the small box he'd been holding behind his back. "Mac. Will you wear my something like a class ring?"

She looked down at the box in her hand and opened it to reveal a gold chain with a heart-shaped padlock and keys. She looked at Finn, her eyes filled with tears. "This is a lot more serious than a class ring."

"Yes, it is. I love you, Mac." Finn leaned in and kissed her. "Will you wear it? Please?"

"I can't believe you love me."

"Of course I love you. What's not to believe. You're sweet, and beautiful, and sexy and you keep my dick hard just by being in the general vicinity, you are a talented musician, and you make me so very, very happy."

"But—"

"Enough with the self-doubt. Will you wear it?"

"Of course I'll wear it."

Finn took the chain from the box and placed it around Mac's neck. He kissed her as he clicked the lock in place. "I think you may be paying for making me wait like that when you already knew your answer."

"In what currency?"

"Oh, you are awfully feisty this Christmas Eve."

"I'm excited. It's time for Santa to open a gift from his sub."

Mac ran out of the room and returned moments later sporting a Santa hat and carrying an exquisitely wrapped box. "Here."

Finn took the box and untied the ribbon.

"Hurry up."

"Patience, elf. It's my present and I will open it in my own time." He picked at the tape and carefully removed the paper. It was too lovely to tear, especially since it came from his first gift from Mac. He already planned to use it next time he gave her a present. He wasn't embarrassed to be sentimental about such things.

He opened the lid. Inside lay a set of black leather wrist and ankle cuffs inlaid with little red hearts. He looked up at Mac and cocked an eyebrow.

"Okay, so it's kind of a twist on how a guy buys a woman lingerie, but it's really a present for him."

"You need to be absolutely clear with me about what these mean, love, because there is no room for error."

"I want you to restrain me while we have every kind of sex."

"Honey, we've only just started having sex of any kind. Yes, it's been going fabulously, and I'm all for you pushing your boundaries, but don't you think it's a little soon to be adding bondage and exotic flavours to the menu?"

"I need to try. If I can do this, then everything else should be a walk in the park, don't you think?"

"No. I don't think. I'm not saying no to trying this, but you need to understand that conquering something near the top of your scary list doesn't mean that everything below it will no longer be scary or a potential issue."

"Yeah, I get that. I suppose, I'm a little high from all my successes and maybe letting them go to my head."

"I want you to celebrate every success you have in whatever way works for you. Just know that I'll be here when I think you need a voice of reason."

"Does this mean we can try?"

"Yes, but in addition to your safewords, you're going to hold a ball in each hand. If either ball drops, its the same as saying red. Everything stops and I get you free. Clear?"

"Clear."

"Safewords?"

Yellow for a minute or to make a change, red to bail."

"Good. And the added safety feature?"

"If I drop either ball, it's the same as saying red."

"Good girl. When I get upstairs, I want to see you laying on your back, and naked on the bed. I want your arms above your head and your legs spread wide. You've got five minutes. Go."

He wondered if she realised her real Christmas gift to him was her trust. Now he had to go upstairs and not fuck it up. No pressure.

MAC MOSTLY OBEYED Finn's order. She lay naked and splayed on his bed, but she kept bringing a hand to her neck so she could fondle her collar. She knew that's what it was, and she intended to get him to call it that before the night was out. What a crazy month it'd been. She felt almost like Jack in the box. Each revolution of the handle conquered another fear. She wondered if this would be the revolution where the top popped open and she sprung out. Free.

"While you aren't lying exactly as I told you, it is Christmas, and you are only disobeying to fondle your—"

Mac didn't wait for him to use that silly euphemism again. "Collar. It's a collar and you can call it what it is. I won't suffer an attack of the vapours."

"Yes, it's a collar. You like it?"

"Very much."

"Good. You may continue to fondle it until I am ready to cuff that wrist. In the meantime, here's how it's going to go. You'll stay on your back the whole time. I'm going to cuff you and clip you to the corners of the bed. I've decided I'm a bit peckish, so I'll be having a little Mac-snack. If all goes well, then I'll feed you some cock. When I've decided you've had enough, I'm going to slide my cock into your cunt for a while. The finale will be my cock in your ass while your pussy is full of Rabbit. You get to have an 'all you can come' night as your reward. Do you still want to try?"

Mac didn't know how she could be so terrified and excited at the same time. She wanted to try, but even though she'd said all kinds of sex, she didn't think that Finn would plan an all inclusive buffet. And anal? She hadn't considered that one. Maybe Finn was right and she was being a little ambitious. "Yellow."

"Okay, what do you need?"

"I don't know about anal."

"What don't you know?"

"I'm scared. I know we do stuff that hurts, but it's a good hurt. Anal was a bad hurt."

"Okay. Think back. Was it only anal that was a bad hurt, or did he hurt your pussy too?"

"Both."

"You trusted me not to hurt your pussy, and how's that working out for you?"

Mac cocked her head slightly and shrugged. "Pretty good."

"I'll take that. You have safewords and ball dropping as an added safety feature, right?"

"Yeah."

"So, do you think you can trust me enough to try? There's no wrong answer, love. I know you trust me. We're talking about one thing that scares you, and not trusting me with that right now is okay. You've already come such a long way in such a short time. Whatever you decide is perfect."

"You won't do anything from behind?"

"Not a thing. You'll be able to see me the whole time."

"Then I want to try."

"Brave girl. I'm going to start with your legs." Finn reached into the box and extracted the larger pair of cuffs. He was slow and deliberate as he attached them, planting a kiss on each ankle before clipping it to a corner of the foot-board. "Colour?"

"Green."

"Good." Finn reached to the floor and pulled a ball from the toy bag he'd set there when he came in, and placed it in Mac's left hand. He fastened a cuff to her wrist and kissed it before clipping it to the left corner of the headboard. He reached into his bag for another ball. He gently disengaged Mac's right hand from her collar and placed the ball in her palm. "Colour?"

"Green."

"Excellent." He fastened the remaining cuff and kissed her wrist before he clipped it to the headboard. He rested his forehead on hers for a moment. "Colour, love?"

"Green."

"Safewords?"

"Yellow for a minute or change, red to bail. If I drop a ball, it means red."

"You've been such a good girl this year, Santa has a nice treat for his sub." Finn kissed his way down Mac's body, stopping to suck on a nipple, giving it a sharp nip before doing the same to the other.

Mac arched her back and clenched the muscles in her pussy in answer to the zing that travelled straight from her nipple to her cunt. "Oh shit, Finn."

"Are you saying you'd like more?"

"Please."

"Not this time, love. Santa still has a treat to deliver." Finn kissed his way down to Mac's belly button, then shifted himself between her legs and licked from the bottom of her weeping slit to her clit, where he lingered, tickling random patterns over it with the tip of his tongue.

Mac moaned and lifted her hips upward, seeking more. Finn adjusted, allowing only feather-light contact between tongue and clit. He circled her entrance with a finger a few times before sliding in and playing with her G-spot.

The man was infuriating. "Pleeeease," Mac whimpered, frantically bucking her hips.

Finn reached up with his free hand and gave her nipple

a rough pinch. "Be a good girl and hold still. You'll get what you need."

Finn continued teasing her until her pussy was dribbling down to her asshole. He lubricated his pinky with her fluid before pressing the very tip of it against her rosette. He took her clit into his mouth, and sucked in time with his finger-strokes to her G-spot until she was on the verge of coming. As she went over, he steadily eased his pinky in her ass up to his third knuckle and held it perfectly still, slipping it out again as her orgasm subsided. "Colour, love?"

"Christmas tree green."

"Good to know. I don't usually like to deviate from the originally scheduled programme, but I think I'll make an exception. While you're sucking my cock, you may have the Rabbit, provided you also have your ass plugged."

"If it means more orgasms, I can be flexible."

"Good girl." Finn grabbed the Rabbit and lube from the bedside table before reaching into the toy-bag for a small butt plug. He slid the Rabbit into her sodden pussy and set it on low. "How are you doing, love?"

"I'd like an orgasm now."

He snapped the lid of lube open and squirted a dollop on his fingers. "Patience, sweetheart." He spread it around her anus and easily sneaked his pinky in and out. He squeezed more into his palm and slathered it all over the plug before placing it at her back entrance. He increased the speed on the Rabbit and applied steady pressure to the plug until it was fully seated. "Colour, love?"

With the Rabbit driving Mac towards a nice big orgasm, she barely noticed the plug as it slid inside her. "Still really green."

"I'm so proud of you." Finn withdrew from between Mac's legs and kissed his way back up her body, taking extra time and care with her nipples. "I want to clamp these, but tonight is only about pleasure. We'll leave pain for another time."

He straddled her chest, wedging his thighs beneath her up-stretched arms so his cock was directly in front of her face. He placed a hand behind Mac's skull and tilted her head forward while he grasped the base of his cock with the other. "Open." Mac's lips parted and Finn slowly fed his cock into her eager mouth.

"Mmm, that feels good, baby." He slid most of the way out. "Now suck hard." He gave a few quick, shallow pumps before he eased his way in, almost to her tonsils, then he held still. "Swallow, and don't stop until I tell you, love."

With each swallow, he barely nudged the tip of his cock against the back of her throat before retreating again, careful to avoid making her gag. When she started moaning, he knew it was time to move on and he gradually pulled his shaft free of her mouth. "So good, love, but I don't want to come yet. I've a couple more places I need to be. Colour?"

"I'm still green."

"Excellent. I can see you're a little tied up, so I guess I'll have to dress myself for the occasion." He lifted his leg over to get off Mac's chest, snagged a condom, and rolled it on.

He checked the circulation in Mac's hands and feet then knelt between her legs. "Right love, the plug stays, but I'll be filling in for the Rabbit. Colour?"

"Nice and green."

He turned the Rabbit off and set it to the side. "Wonderful. Would you like to come?"

"Boy would I ever."

"Good." She moaned and clenched her teeth as he slid

inside. He latched onto her right thigh for leverage as he thrust deep. He snatched the bullet and set it buzzing against her clit. He was tempted to let her come now, but he really wanted her good and needy before he tried to fuck her ass. He considered for a moment, then decided not to stretch this session out much longer. She'd been such a trouper and he wanted the night to end on a high note. He removed the bullet and withdrew his cock. "It's time, baby. Colour?"

"Not so green."

"Are you yellow, love?"

"Not quite."

"Let's talk for a minute then. What are you scared of?"

"Bad hurt."

"Have I given you any bad hurt tonight?"

"Yes."

Finn raised a single eyebrow at her. "What was bad hurt and why didn't you say anything?"

"You pinched my nipple, but I knew I deserved it."

Finn chuckled. Okay. Was that really bad hurt, or are you just stalling?"

"Stalling," she confessed. "You didn't really give me any bad hurt."

"And how are you feeling with the plug?"

"Weird, but it doesn't hurt."

"I'm bigger than the plug, but I will do everything I can to keep you from feeling bad hurt, okay?"

"I know. You promised me tonight was all I can come, and I'm sure I can come more than this."

"I'll make sure you get to come as much as you want. I bet I'll even make you come while I'm fucking your ass."

"I bet you won't."

"You're on. What do you want if you win?"

"If I don't come while you're fucking my ass, you don't ever get to fuck it again."

"Alright, but if I do make you come while fucking your ass, you have to wear the butt plug of my choice all day tomorrow, and I get to fuck your ass any time I want."

"I don't know, you sound way too confident."

"Do we have a deal, or not? The longer you stall, the longer you have to wait for your orgasms."

"Deal."

"Brave girl. Too bad you're going to lose. I have just the plug in mind for you tomorrow."

"I'll take my chances. My luck's been holding out pretty well so far."

"We'll see. Colour?"

"Green."

"Here we go then." Finn replaced the Rabbit in Mac's pussy and turned it on the lowest setting. He squeezed a large puddle of lube into his palm and coated his cock thoroughly. Then he carefully removed the plug and positioned the lube at her anus and squeezed some into her rectum before inserting a finger to spread it around. He positioned the tip of his cock and paused. "Colour, love?"

"Green," she squeaked.

"Good girl. Push out as I push in. It'll make things go much smoother." Finn flipped the switch and increased the Rabbit's speed and leaned in, using the weight of his body to provide steady pressure. "Breathe, baby, you need to breathe. Slow, steady breaths, in and out. Almost there, love." As he felt her slight push, he leaned a little harder, and there it was, that pop of cock breaching ass. "Colour love?"

"Yellow."

"Okay, we're going to rest for a minute and let you get

used to it. The hardest part is over, you know. The head is inside you. Any pain?"

She paused before answering. "No. A little burn, but no bad pain."

"Perfect. It'll feel nothing but good, really soon, I promise."

"You and your damn promises."

"Colour?"

"I'm closing in on green."

"Excellent." Finn resumed his steady pressure and kept going until his body was flush with hers. "There we go, baby. All in. Still green?"

"Yes."

"Then, it's orgasm time." He increased the speed on the vibrator and pulled out leaving just the head inside. He drizzled more lube over his cock and pushed back in to the hilt and held for a moment as he studied Mac's face. She had an almost serene smile on her face and she still held the balls in her hands. He braced his hands on her hips and withdrew to the head one more time before he was certain she was ready for him to fuck her. He pumped in and out, his momentum increasing with each thrust.

Mac threw her head back and let out a high-pitched whine as her hips gyrated and her legs shook.

With Mac in the throes of her orgasm, Finn picked up the pace, hammering at her furiously. When she came again, he let go and erupted with such intensity, he was a little concerned for the integrity of the condom. "Colour, love?"

"Holly jolly green."

"Perfect. I'm going to pull out and get you loose. Then I'll be back to clean you up." He bit back a sigh of relief as he pulled out and saw the condom had survived the encounter. He unclipped Mac's restraints and gave her a quick kiss on the lips before retreating to the bathroom to dispose of the condom and grab a warm, damp cloth. He was surprised to feel a hand on his back, and turned to see Mac sporting a huge grin. "You were supposed to stay put and I was going to come and take care of you."

"I thought a shower together would be better."

"I love the way you think, baby."

"I love you, Finn."

Finn stared at Mac for a moment, a little stunned. Somewhere inside, he was sure she loved him, but he didn't think she was ready to say it out loud. He swung her off her feet as he grabbed her in a tight hug and said, "I love you too, Mac," before he kissed her silly.

***

MAC CHECKED THE CALLER ID, and grinned as she answered, "Merry Christmas, Sully." She shifted, trying to find a comfortable position. She almost yelped when the plug in her ass started vibrating, and she silently vowed never to bet against Finn again.

"Merry Christmas, gorgeous. Was Santa good to you?"

"Santa was very good to me. And so were you. I don't know how to thank you for always giving me exactly what I needed at precisely the right time."

"It's a Dom thing. As for thanking me, how about letting me off the hook for those two favours to be named later?"

"No way, there is not a sub on the planet who would give up unspecified favours from a Dom. Best Christmas ever."

One Gold Knot (Dominant Cord, Book 2)

She didn't do relationships. She didn't even do all night.

After years of avoiding her teenage crush, Hildy Klein is shocked to come face to face with Wilson Kennedy.

Her uncle's wake isn't the place to unravel all the ways that Wilson could leave her emotionally vulnerable and exposed, yet his gentle persistence is impossible to ignore.

But Wilson is no longer that boy in her fantasies, and now Hildy must decide if she will give up control and commit to the protective, kinky Dom he's become.

ONE GOLD KNOT

CHAPTER ONE

Wilson did a double take at the sign on the back of the Smart Car parked in front of The Squeaky Wheel, not sure he'd read it right. He turned to Sully and raised a brow. "Newly Dead?"

Sully chuckled. "Erich's instructions for his wake were frustratingly detailed."

They stomped the snow from their feet and entered the pub. Wilson immediately spotted the other members of their wind quintet, Dominant Cord, at the bar. He snagged Sully's sleeve and gently pulled him along as he went to join the group.

"Hey guys, we finally made it."

"Hi Wil, I was getting a little concerned," Finn said.

"Blame Sully. I had to drive like my grandmother because our delicate flower bitched and complained about his sore ribs."

Mac snorted and rolled her eyes. "Good grief, Sully. I don't know how you're supposed to be ready to play the upcoming concerts if you can't even handle a car-ride without whining."

"Geez, what does it take for a guy to get a little sympathy?"

"You could stop letting your cock make your dating decisions."

"Well, I'd never been ice-skating before, and it sounded like fun—"

Shaking her head in obvious disbelief, Mac interrupted. "Bullshit, Sully. You just wanted to touch her feet. Too bad you broke your ribs before you had the chance to be the perfect gentleman and help remove her skates."

Wilson lost interest in the conversation. While banter between Mac and Sully was generally entertaining, he was fed up with hearing about Sully's injury. He let his eyes wander, and the lone woman in the back corner of the room caught his attention. Hildy. He'd only met her that one time, years ago, but she snuck into his dreams with disturbing regularity. Her demeanour screamed stay away, but her haunted look made him want to scoop her into his arms and comfort her. "I'll be back later."

Griff followed his gaze and said, "Yeah, good luck with that."

Wilson crossed the floor, never once taking his eyes off his quarry.

The moment Wilson turned from the bar and caught her eye, Hildy was positive the universe was a sadistic asshole.

When he'd walked in with Sully earlier, her stomach hit the floor and her heart raced so fast she thought she might black out. She couldn't believe her good fortune when he'd headed straight to the bar without so much as a side-ways glance.

Deep down, she knew he'd come, no matter how hard

she tried to convince herself otherwise. It was bad enough she had to be here and say goodbye to the one person in her family who loved her — she didn't need her teenage crush bearing witness to her all-consuming grief, too.

Her only option now was to gain the upper-hand and get rid of him. She looked him in the eye. "Hello Wilson. Is there something I can help you with?"

"Hey, Hildy," he smiled and offered his hand, "it's been a long time, I didn't think you'd remember me."

Remember? How could she forget? That day was branded on her soul. Every night since then, she imagined she was swaddled in his arms instead of her blanket. And she always fucked with her eyes closed so she could pretend Wil was the one she was with.

Her mind drifted back to her fifteen year old self. Back then, she practised on her uncle's piano because her parents had sold hers when she stopped being their performing monkey. They'd been livid when she'd stood before that capacity crowd and made her apologies as she announced her immediate retirement.

She stamped down her outrage and forced her thoughts back to the day she met Wilson. Normally, she was long gone before students arrived for their lessons, but she'd been learning a new piece and was oblivious to her surroundings until her uncle placed a gentle hand on her shoulder.

Hildy nodded. "Yeah, I remember. My uncle cajoled me into accompanying you, and afterwards, you walked me to the library." That wasn't all he'd done that afternoon. He'd touched her, held her, oh, and he'd kissed her. She'd been emotionally ill-equipped to handle the unfamiliar feelings, and she'd successfully avoided further contact with him. Until now.

"That's right." Wilson's smile morphed into that irresistible lop-sided grin. He paused, his eyes swept across the empty table top and then back to her face. "How about I grab us a drink and we can catch up?"

Hildy silently cursed temptation and lied. "If you don't mind, I'd prefer to be on my own."

Wilson lifted an eyebrow. "Are you positive?"

From the corner of her eye Hildy saw the elderly couple walk in. Fuck. Georg and Martha. The universe was definitely not on her side today. They headed straight for her and she needed Wilson gone. Now. She'd survived a lot over the years, but she couldn't handle being humiliated by them in front of the only guy she'd ever met who could matter. "Absolutely. Now, if you don't mind...?"

To her horror, he pulled out the chair next her and sat. Then it was too late. They stood before her, and she couldn't do anything but ride out the oncoming shit-storm.

"Brunehilde." She could hear the sneer in his voice, and she tried not to cringe at the use of her full name. "I should have known you'd show up where you're not welcome. But then, you never were a smart girl, so I'll spell it out for you in short, simple words. Get the fuck out, you selfish cunt." Hildy stared blankly at the wall and mentally assumed the fetal position, prepared for the rest of Georg's tirade.

"That's enough. Nobody speaks to Hildy like that. Go find somewhere else to spew your toxic feculence." It was Wilson's dangerously quiet voice that yanked Hildy from her safe place. She looked over to see her uninvited guest had risen to his feet, towering over the couple as he upbraided them.

"How dare you," Martha sputtered, "is that how you were taught to speak to your elders?"

"No, this is how I was taught to stick up for someone

who is being bullied. Age, gender, and relationship are irrelevant."

Hildy could barely keep her jaw off the floor. The only person who ever effectively stood up to them in her defence was dead.

"Well, I never. I don't need to stand here and be insulted like this. Come on Georg, let's go find somewhere to sit." Martha dragged Georg with her as she stalked off towards an empty table.

Sully arrived moments later. "I'm sorry, sweetie, I got side-tracked. Are you okay? They weren't invited, but I should have known they'd show up anyway."

"I'm fine." Hildy angled her head towards Wilson. "Besides, your buddy here delivered a most righteous smack-down."

Sully grinned. "Damn, and I missed it."

"Yes, you did. I might fill you in on the all the juicy details over dinner one night this week, if you're buying." Hildy batted her eyelashes and shot Sully a cheeky smile.

"Deal. Now, I've got to get this show on the road." Sully leaned in to give Hildy a kiss on the cheek and whispered, "I know you need some space, but let him stay, sweets. Trust me."

"I'll consider it."

"Good enough. You're up first. I figured you'd prefer to get it all done and out of the way."

After all these years, she shouldn't be surprised at his ability to anticipate her needs. Her uncle taught him well. She choked back her tears. "Thank you."

As he was leaving, Sully pointed to Wilson and said, "Trust. Me."

Wilson's gentle touch on her shoulder felt nice in a way that still scared her. "Hildy, what can I do?"

Dammit, she needed him to go away. "Look, I appreciate you sticking up for me, but I can take care of myself. Now, if you don't mind, I really do want to be left alone"

"Hildy, whether you realise it or not, what you want is not necessarily what you need. I'll sit here quietly and you can pretend to be alone if you like, but you need a buffer."

"Why do men always think they know what's best for me?"

"Honey, I just watched you disappear inside yourself. I wouldn't leave anyone open to more of that kind of abuse. It's clear you're hurting, and I only want to give you a safe environment in which to cope. Can you let me do that?"

She was torn, but her intense urge to run home and bundle up in her blanket was eclipsed by love and respect for her uncle. She had come emotionally prepared to deal with Georg and Martha, but this handsome, kind, annoying man had thrown her off, and now she felt vulnerable. Wilson's voice interrupted her inner turmoil.

"Stop, you're going to give yourself an aneurysm. Just breathe. I'm going to get you some water, but before I leave, I'm going to give you a quick kiss on the lips because I think an implied relationship might help keep those asshats at bay."

Hildy didn't have time to respond before his lips grazed her own. All those lonely nights she lay awake remembering the feel of his kisses did nothing to prepare her for the riot this one incited between her thighs. It was the first good feeling she'd had in days. She stole glance at Martha and Georg, and took some perverse pleasure at their indignant scowls. Maybe company wasn't a bad idea. Besides, he was still awfully pretty to look at, and maybe she'd score another kiss or two. She wished she could take him home for a good fuck, but he was her long-time crush and she didn't do relationships. Hell, she didn't even do all night, and she was willing to bet he did both.

"Here you go."

Hildy snapped out of her daydream and managed a small smile for Wilson as he set the water in front of her. "Thank you."

He trailed a finger down her cheek. "You're welcome."

His small gesture created a big wet spot in her panties and an even bigger lump in her belly. She didn't know how to process touching like this. Too scary. A kiss would have been better. She could handle kissing. Fuck, company was such a bad idea. "You haven't asked me who they are."

"No, I haven't. Like everything else, you'll tell me when you're ready. Now, hush. I promised to just sit here and let you be."

Ready? She was never ready, but she'd opened the door, and it was time to shove Wilson through it. "Not your typical meet the parents, was it?"

"Your parents? Are you fucking shitting me?"

Hildy cringed slightly before straightening and lifting her chin. "I wish I were, but there it is. I didn't even rate a booby prize in the parent lottery."

"I guess not, and I'm sorry for that." Wilson cupped her cheek and leaned in for another kiss. "It looks like things are going to get started soon. Is there anything you need before it gets crazy?"

What the fuck? People couldn't dump her fast enough after meeting her parents. This was one man Hildy did not know how to handle. He said and did all the right things. How could he possibly know what she needed when she didn't even know herself?

"No, thank you. My uncle asked me to come out of retirement and perform tonight, just for him. It's been a long time since I've had an audience, so, I'm going to need a few minutes to myself to get my head screwed on straight."

"Whatever you need."

Hildy took some deep breaths in an effort to calm down. Damn Uncle Erich anyway for making her promise to do this. Why did he have to get sick and die? Life was so fucking unfair. She didn't realise she was crying until she felt the tears being wiped from her face. She looked at Wilson and tried to smile.

"It's okay, sweetie, you go ahead and let it out."

"Later. I'll let it out later. I really do need to get my shit together. The worst thing I can do is fuck this up with my parents right there."

Wilson stroked her cheek as he gazed into her eyes. "What's your favourite colour?"

"What?"

He winked and shot her that sexy lopsided grin of his. "Work with me here."

Against her better judgement, Hildy gave in and played along. "Dark purple, what's yours?"

"That pretty shade of hazel I see when I look into your eyes."

"Feeding me lines of bullshit is not helpful."

"Sweetheart, I don't bullshit. Ever. Favourite thing to have for supper?"

"Hmmm," Hildy tapped her chin as she considered, "chicken sandwiches with mayonnaise and cranberry sauce."

Wilson laughed. "That's lunch."

"It's whatever I want it to be. So there." Hildy grinned and stuck her tongue out.

"You're awfully cheeky. If you were mine, there might be consequences for display like that."

"Well, I'm not yours." Hildy paused, then curiosity got the better of her. "But if I were, what kind of consequences?"

"Oh honey, this is not the kind of conversation I had in mind. Not yet, anyway."

Hildy had known Sully her whole life; she knew precisely what sorts of shenanigans his quintet got up to in Finn's basement, and she had a pretty good idea what Wilson meant by consequences. Surprisingly, she found the prospect arousing, but Wil was right about this not being where her head should be right now. She squeezed her legs together and tried not to squirm, but that wet spot in her panties kept growing.

Her focus shifted as Sully's voice drifted through the sound system. "May I have your attention, everyone." Once the room was silent, he continued, "We're here to celebrate the life of Erich Klein. I know most of you were unaware of his illness, and his death came as a shock. That's how he wanted it. Shortly before he died, Erich sat me down and gave me a long list of orders to be executed upon his death and threatened to haunt me silly if I didn't. Needless to say, the miserable bugger has kept me hopping from the moment he kicked the bucket.

"As you can see," Sully pointed at the glass box on the bar, "I've burnt the body, but only because I couldn't convince the undertaker to embalm him with good single malt scotch. Make sure you have a drink with him and tell him a funny story.

"Erich had three absolute loves in his life. Ted, music, and Hildy. He lost Ted in their third year of university, back when gay-bashing wasn't a hate-crime. With Ted gone, he buried himself in the deepest part of the closet, music his only joy. Then Hildy came along and filled the hole in his heart.

"At Erich's request, Hildy has agreed perform *Gounod's Funeral March of a Marionette*. For the non-music geeks here today, you may recognise it as the theme music from the TV show, *Alfred Hitchcock Presents*."

Hildy had known this moment was coming for days, but she still felt woefully unprepared. As she stood, Wilson took her hand and kissed her knuckles. "You'll be fine sweetheart. I'll be right here when you're done."

Hildy forced herself towards the piano. Her heart was broken, but her uncle didn't want her to be sad. She thought back to all his other seemingly impossible edicts, and almost smiled. As she reached the performance area, Sully gave her a gentle hug and whispered, "It'll be fine. He loved you. Now give him everything you've got."

Before settling at the piano, Hildy looked up into Sully's watery eyes. "Thanks."

As soon as she played the first notes, the people and the room no longer existed for her. There was only the piano, and the music. The tightness in her chest eased, and she felt just a little less sad. Her uncle had an uncanny ability to give her what she needed. Even in death.

Wilson watched as Hildy poured herself into the music. He thought back to the unforgivable way her parents treated her. He stole a glance at the couple in question and wasn't surprised to see them sporting identical scowls. Fuck 'em.

He was glad he'd made that split-second decision to shield Hildy from that noxious pair of wank-stains, and he didn't consider it a hardship to continue. That glint in her eye when she asked him about consequences was promising. He wasn't opposed to a little funishment. Damn. Her long legs and luscious lips had him more than interested, but the way she caressed that piano made him wish his cock were the ivory beneath her fingers. No doubt every other man in the room had similar thoughts.

With the decay of the final note, Wilson hurried to meet Hildy and escort her back to their table. His drive to protect her was strong, but the broken look on her face during the incident with her parents had him almost feral.

Sully thanked Hildy, and Wilson gathered her close, planting a kiss the top of her head. "That was beautiful, love." He kept his arm around her as he guided her along. Before she could take her seat, he parked himself on his own and pulled her onto his lap. He was quick to wrap his arms around her and tuck her head beneath his chin. He breathed easy once he felt her body relax. "There you go, sweetheart, just rest." With a nod of reassurance to Sully, Wilson hugged Hildy a little tighter and rocked her back and forth as she sobbed. "Let it out, love, I've got you, and I'll keep you safe."

Sully headed towards Wilson and Hildy as soon as he finished introducing the next performance. "Is she okay, Wil?"

"She will be. Right now she needs a cuddle and good cry."

"Agreed. Should I make other arrangements for getting home?"

"Nope, I'm a firm believer in leave with the one ya brung. That said, I think we'll be in charge of making sure Hildy gets home safely."

Hildy pulled her head back from Wilson's body. "I am perfectly capable of getting myself home safely, thank you very much."

Sully reached out and stroked her hair. "Nobody is

saying otherwise, sweetheart, but it's been a difficult, emotional day, and unfortunately, it's likely to get worse before it gets better. I need you to trust me when I tell you it will get much, much better, but for now, let us support you, okay?"

With a long sigh, Hildy gave in. "Okay. I'm too wrung out to argue."

"Promise?"

"I promise."

"Good girl. Wil, I have to go up there and do more official stuff…"

"No worries, I've got her back. One thing, though. Can you give Mac a heads-up on the situation? I don't want Hildy to be alone anywhere, and I can't be with her if she needs the facilities."

"No need, she caught that little encounter with the cum infested pus bubbles and was all set to kick some ass. Your way was likely more elegant, but hers is always worth the price of admission."

"I'll die a happy man if I get through the rest of my life without feeling the sharp-side of her tongue."

"Good luck with that. Oops, that's my cue. Gotta go. Hildy, remember, Wilson is here to lean on, and you promised."

Hildy nodded and buried herself in Wilson's arms. He kissed the top of her head before resting his cheek there.

Wilson opened the front passenger door of his car. "In you get, Hildy. Sully can sit in the back."

"I don't mind taking the back seat. Sully's injured, so he should get the front."

"Not a chance, I had to put up with him in the front

the whole way here. He's notorious for back-seat driving, so he may as well be appropriately located."

"I thought you liked me, Wilson," Sully complained.

"I do like you, but given the choice between a hot woman and you sitting next me, you're going to lose every single time."

Hildy's face flushed and she dropped her gaze to the ground.

"Now look what you did," Sully accused.

"It's fine, Sully, really. Stop fussing. One minute you act like Wilson is the best thing that could possibly happen to me, and the next you're behaving like he's an axe-murderer."

"You know me, I'm not happy unless I'm fussing."

"Well, yeah, but stop it." Hildy demanded.

"Get in the car. I hurt, and I want to go home."

"Oh god." Wilson turned to Hildy. "Do you mind if we drop Sully off first? I'd like to get home before dawn."

Hildy chuckled. "Nope, I'm all for self-preservation, and this will minimise how much complaining we both have to endure."

"Seriously? You too, Hildy?"

"Oh, suck it up, you big baby," Wilson ordered. "It's been almost six weeks since you broke those ribs. If you can't handle a ride in the car, how do you expect to be ready to play in time for all the Valentine's gigs?"

"I'll manage just fine as long as you don't add to the damage now."

"Oh for fuck's sake. Get in the back and be quiet or we'll visit every pot-hole and speed bump in the city before I drop you right back here and you can get a cab home." Wilson lifted his eyebrows. "Still want to bitch about my driving?"

Sully clamped his lips shut and slid into the back of the car.

Hildy sniggered. "Thanks, Wilson. I am SO making a special note of this. I don't think I've ever seen anyone shut Sully up so effectively without a ball-gag."

"Ball-gag? Tell me it's true and there is photographic evidence." Wilson glanced up at the rear-view mirror for Sully's reaction. Nothing. Damn him and that inscrutable face of his. He turned his head for a quick look at Hildy and not only knew she told the truth, but whip poker with her would be oodles of fun. "Well, is there?"

"No comment," Hildy said as she turned her face towards the passenger side window.

Wilson snuck another quick glance in the rear-view mirror, and was sure he saw a flash of relief in Sully's eyes. Interesting. This would be worth pursuing.

The ride to Sully's place was quiet and uneventful, but once Sully was safely indoors, that changed. Wilson drove a few blocks and parked the car. He turned to Hildy, and with a penetrating stare, he began his interrogation.

"You had to know I wouldn't let this one go, so I suggest you give in gracefully and tell me all there is to know about Sully wearing a ball-gag."

"I have nothing to tell you."

Wilson's eyes flashed. "That's complete bullshit. Let's get one thing straight, right now. You do not lie to me. Ever. Not even little tiny white ones meant to avoid hurt feelings. Are we clear?"

"You're in no position to make demands of me. In addition, Mr. Hypocrite, you sit there and tell me never to lie to you, but your implication of a relationship to keep Martha and Georg off my back sure smells like a lie to me."

"True, it was certainly a lie by implication, but I lied to a pair of bullies with whom I have no obligation of trust so I could protect a woman with whom I am interested in exploring a trusting relationship."

"Look, while I appreciate what you did to protect me, our implied relationship ended the moment we left the Squeaky Wheel. Now, if you don't mind, I'm tired and I'd like to go home."

"Regardless of whether we're romantically involved or not, we now have a relationship of a sort, and I will accept nothing less than the truth from you."

"Our relationship, whatever it may be, ends the moment I get out of this car, which will be here and now if we're not moving in the next ten seconds."

"Hold on..."

"Eight...seven..."

Wilson started the car and eased onto the road. "Can we at least talk whilst I'm driving?"

"No. I just want to get home. It's been a long, tedious day."

"Okay, quiet it is."

Wilson briefly considered taking the long way to Hildy's house in case she might be tempted to engage in some conversation, but if he were to have any chance with her, he needed to play it completely straight. Even in the silence, the ten minutes it took to get Hildy home sped by too quickly and left Wilson wanting more.

"Thanks for the ride."

"You're welcome, sweetheart." Wilson got out of the car along with Hildy.

"What are you doing?"

"Making sure you get home safely. Just go with it and let me be the gentleman my mother thinks she raised."

Hildy rolled her eyes and sped up the path to her house, Wilson keeping pace beside her. Once Hildy had the door open, Wilson placed his hands on her upper arms and gently turned her towards him. "Since our relationship is about to turn into a pumpkin, may I please have one last kiss?"

"Good grief, Wilson, will you give it up already?"

"I'm persistent. It's one of my many redeeming qualities."

"Oh, what the hell. One kiss."

Wilson gathered Hildy into his arms. He touched his lips her forehead, her nose, and finally to her lips before trailing his tongue along the seam of her mouth. She opened to him and he deepened the kiss, tangling his tongue with hers in between teasing sucks and nips. When Wilson finally eased way from Hildy, he studied her face and smiled. She was just as affected. "What time shall I pick you up in the morning to get your car?"

"You don't need to do that. I can manage on my own."

"I won't leave you stranded for tomorrow. So, what time would you like me to pick you up in the morning?"

Hildy huffed. "Can you be here by eight-fifteen? I have a student at nine."

"I'll be here. Goodnight, sweetheart. Now, go inside and lock the door. I'm not moving from this spot until you do."

"You are awfully bossy."

"It comes with the territory. You'll get used to it."

"Cocky much?"

"Go."

"Alright, I'm going, I'm going."

Once he heard the deadbolt snick into place, Wilson returned to his car and headed home. He'd known she'd be at Erich's wake, but he hadn't been prepared for how intensely attracted he still was to her. He thought back to that afternoon when they were teenagers. He was pretty sure he'd been her first kiss. Damn, he'd wanted to be her first everything, but he never saw her again. He didn't need to be her first anymore, but he did want to be her only.

One Gold Triquetra (Dominant Cord, Book 3)

A decade ago, a bad play-date turned composer Ella Hudson off BDSM.

Now she's been offered a performance opportunity too good to pass up, but it means working closely with Jackson and Griffin--world class musicians, lovers, and Doms intent on adding her to their relationship.

While Ella struggles to deny her true desires, maintaining her vanilla facade becomes increasingly difficult as the men re-introduce her to a world she'd written off.

Tainted Pearl: A Rock Star Prequel

Lust at first sight has never been a problem for Doug Fraser before, but something about Biddy O'Mara screams "hands off". Except the private, mysterious musician is also the sexiest, most captivating woman he's ever crammed into close quarters with.

Biddy can't afford any distractions while on a month long eco-activism island adventure. The rock star is incognito for a very good cause, but the irresistible camera operator quickly proves a big, bad complication.

A fling is inevitable. But Doug's not relationship material, and the more he gets to know Biddy, the more he realizes she's the type of girl you take home to meet your mother—even if you don't know all her secrets.

Tainted Shadow (Tainted Pearl, Book 1)

Tainted Pearl's lead singer has a stalker problem and bodyguard Brody Clarke doesn't think twice about cutting his vacation short when he's asked to protect her.

Sparks fly—and not the good kind—when he rubs the rabidly independent rock star the wrong way. Now he needs to convince her that letting him be in control might just save her life.

And if it has the side benefit of turning those sparks into a completely different kind of heat? Brody's up for that kind of dominance as well.

Prime Minster (Frisky Beavers #1)

Gavin:

Ellie Montague is smart, sensitive, and so gorgeous it hurts to look at her. She's also an intern in my office. The office of the Prime Minister of Canada.*

That's me. The PM.

She calls me that because when she calls me Sir, I get hard and she gets flustered, and as long as she's my intern, I can't twist my hands in her strawberry-blonde hair and show her what else I'd like her to do with that pretty pink mouth.**

Ellie:

How much I like the PM varies on a daily basis. He's intense, controlling, and a perfectionist in every way—and he demands the same of his staff.

How much I want him never wavers.

There's something about him that tugs at me deep inside, and makes me wish that just once he'd cross the line in a late night work session. I'd take that secret to the grave if it meant I got a taste of the barely restrained beast inside him.***

FOOTNOTES:

* This is a fictional erotic romance. No prime ministers or interns were harmed in the making of this book.

** Except it's a BDSM romance, so they were hurt a little.

*** Spoiler alert: she gets more than a taste. And she likes it.

ACKNOWLEDGMENTS

Madelynne Ellis for her endless support. Elise Logan for being the first to beta-read and showing me the errors of my way. The wonderful gang of Divas who are generous in so many ways. And of course, my wonderful, supportive husband, who says yes to almost everything...except another dog.

ABOUT THE AUTHOR

Surrounded by mist-covered mountains, Sadie Haller lives a quiet life with her husband and fur-babies.

Where to find Sadie

sadiehaller.com
sadie@sadiehaller.com

www.ingramcontent.com/pod-product-compliance
Lightning Source LLC
Chambersburg PA
CBHW020618120726
47905CB00003B/841